IN THE
DARK DEAD OF NIGHT

The thing from the swamp moved slowly along the shoulder of the asphalt, taking cover in the soft foliage that had usurped the road. Stalking between moonlight and shadow, it was hard to discern. However, it was coming closer to the flashlight and to the two boys crouched around the red motorcycle.

Finally Billy Bob finished pumping the motorcycle tire. He stopped, thumped the tire once, and unscrewed the valve connection. As he stood, the thundering frog chorus that had accompanied him and Sonny through most of the swamp slowed gradually, then stopped as if someone had turned the volume to "off."

Sonny and Billy Bob both tensed. The silence was deafening.

Then another strange, distant, moaning sound rose softly....

SOFTLY WALKS THE BEAST

THOMAS O'D. HUNTER

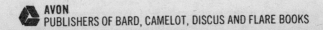

AVON
PUBLISHERS OF BARD, CAMELOT, DISCUS AND FLARE BOOKS

SOFTLY WALKS THE BEAST is an original publication of Avon Books. This work has never before appeared in book form.

AVON BOOKS
A division of
The Hearst Corporation
959 Eighth Avenue
New York, New York 10019

First Avon Printing, December, 1982

AVON TRADEMARK REG. U. S. PAT. OFF. AND IN
OTHER COUNTRIES, MARCA REGISTRADA, HECHO EN
U. S. A.

Printed in the U. S. A.

WFH 10 9 8 7 6 5 4 3 2 1

To my wife, Isabelle, and Dr. John Riedel, my medical adviser. I hope this will do for bomb lovers what VD films did for me in the Marine Corps.

It began as such things always begin—in the ooze of un-noticed swamps, in the darkness of eclipsed moons. It began with a strangled gasping for air.

—Loren Eiseley, *The Immense Journey*

Whoever battles with monsters had better see that it does not turn him into a monster. And if you gaze long into the abyss, the abyss will gaze back into you.

—Friedrich Nietzsche, *Beyond Good and Evil*

A moderately speedy fungus grows a branch (or mycelium) at the rate of an inch per hour. Each advancing branch puts out a new side branch about every half hour or so, and these grow at the same rate. In twenty-four hours, a fungus colony of that kind can produce a total branch length of one-half mile. In forty-eight hours, the total length is hundreds of miles long.

—*Science Digest*, November/December 1980

PROLOGUE

They were out there beyond the capsule door, and he could hear them trying to get to him. Not through the blastproof door itself, because that was made of heavy steel and concrete; but he *could* hear them through the TV intercom. Nails and teeth scratching on the tunnel walls, their awful croaking and moaning—yes, during the first week, he'd been masochistic enough to listen. Even to watch through the security monitors.

To see Captain Brolio's old command looking and acting like that was sickening.

He glanced up quickly, checking the air gauge: one minute, fifty-three seconds and fading. Forcing his head down again, he applied the Bic pen twitching in his fingers to paper.

"Up the fifty-foot ladder they crawl every night," he scrawled in the logbook in a looping, manic hand. Probably to forage for food; plenty of food in the swamp.

He stroked his scrubby new beard. Over two weeks now and they're still alive. I'm almost dead and they're getting stronger. Maybe radiation agrees with them. And his eyes glazed over as he thought about the level of radiation aboveground.

With near total blankness he stared down the length of the

computerized panel, which should have released ten Minute-men missiles in just thirty-two seconds, had the Russians not fouled targeting communications. The near-miss had landed instead on the edge of the Okefenokee; had kicked up all sorts of muck from the swamp; had splattered it right on top of them.

An interesting blend of cocktail dip, he thought whimsically. To a base of rotting, steaming algae and swamp fungus, add billions of our own laboratory germs programmed to kill those few who survive the nuclear holocaust. Microwave at once with intense radioactivity.

Wysinski, an intelligent nineteen-year-old, smiled like a madman.

Try that on a potato chip. Give it to the kids. Watch their eyes run. See their lips turn green with slime. In just three days, you can prune them.

He was fading again, his eyes trying to roll up and shrink into the back of his head. He reached for the last white pill in a small tin box marked "Air Force Amphetamine."

But he never made it. Instead his mind flashed white, his head hit the panel with a blunt thud, and his right hand knocked over the wallet displayed upright like a picture frame.

Forty seconds passed. The red warning light, the one marked "AIR," blinked on and off in time with a computerized bleeper. Then a previously recorded voice slurred on automatically, draining a finite source of energy.

> THIS...IS...A...ONE...MINUTE...
> WARNING....YOU...HAVE...ONE...
> MINUTE...TO...CLEAR...THE...
> MINUTEMAN...CONTROL...CAPSULE.
> ...I...REPEAT...YOU...HAVE...

Wysinski's hand twitched. It tensed against the metal panel. It pushed. Slowly he raised his bewildered head, a young wak-ing child searching for its parents.

He struggled to his unfelt feet.

> THIS...IS...A...WARNING....

His body shook violently. He reached out for his cheap leather wallet. He turned it over to look at the photograph he'd taken with an Instamatic just six months before. His mother and two kid sisters, slightly out of focus, smiled at him from a spotless white kitchen.

He thought he detected an accusation in their smiles. Something that hadn't been there before.

I...REPEAT...YOU...HAVE...THIRTY
...SECONDS...TO...CLEAR...

Wysinski shuddered, his shoulders shaking up and down. Hot tears flowed for his mother. For his two kid sisters. For himself.

He had survived.

By some strange instinct he had locked himself in the control capsule before he'd been infected by the others. He'd been here for over two weeks now, carefully rationing his air. Food gone; no water left; popping Dexedrine to stay awake, alert, writing maudlin poems in his log to a suffocating world.

TWENTY...SECONDS...TO...CLEAR...
THE...MINUTEMAN...CONTROL...

For courage he gnawed on the last pill.

Images rapidly seesawed through his brain: a mad Arab leader nuking the Suez Canal, the Israelis turning the Arabs' desert to glass. Russian outrage, the rogue Air Force general opening midwestern silos against presidential orders, a faulty Russian computer chip. Sweet diplomacy dying at the gentle stroke of her little red button. A first strike, a second strike, no one left to stop it, targets, not cities, not people, not even things...just targets...an approved video game of computerized objectives.

BLAM, BLAM, BLAM...BLAP, BLAP,
BLAP...BLIP, BLIP, BLIP...TEN...
SECONDS ...TO...CLEAR...THE...
MINUTEMAN ...CONTROL...
CAPSULE....

Wysinski turned to look at the heavy metal wheel centered in the capsule door, then, eyes rolling, glanced back to the control panel. His hand reached out, flicked a switch marked SECURITY MONITORS: 1, 2, 3, 4.

The overhead monitors flickered to half life; reception

snowy and warped. But something did move in the murkiness beyond the capsule door. As if to confirm this, Wysinski's hand turned up the volume control.

He heard low, guttural rumblings, an insane scratching of nails against concrete walls.

Yes, they were still waiting.

He flicked off the monitor switch. His breath was noticeably shorter, almost a hiccup. He staggered, fell to his knees, his hand reaching out for the photograph.

He pressed the picture to his lips and kissed it.

No more warning voice. No more time.

He gulped from the lifeless capsule great mouthfuls of his own carbon dioxide. All the fluids leaking from his body had turned his face agate white.

Get out now, he thought, right now. He reeled away from the panel, then crumpled to the green skidproof linoleum deck.

"Oh, mother of God!"

With extraordinary effort he pushed himself up from the floor and threw back his head, eyes tensed shut, tears of desolation—the last of his human reserve—boiling down his bearded cheeks.

"I'm dying."

He crawled toward the capsule door through the human debris: an April *Playboy,* a Hershey bar wrapper, cigarette butts, empty cans of emergency rations.

He reached the hatch door. Pulling himself up to his knees, he gripped the wheel. He forced it counterclockwise. It was heavy, hard to turn without the hydraulics, but somehow he managed. The two-inch bolts slid silently from their jams and retracted into the door itself. Slowly, ever so slowly, the huge mass opened.

With a giant WHOOOOSH, air entered the stagnant capsule.

Wysinski, the drowning man, kneeled in the open doorway, eyes still locked shut, lungs wrenching oxygen from the fetid air, chewing it, digesting it, loving it beyond fear.

Then gradually, imperceptibly, he could hear sounds other than his own breathing. A foot sliding forward. Shuffling and sliding. A low, rumbling reptilian moan.

His eyelids remained frozen, his eyeballs twitching beneath chalk-white membranes.

The ponderous, congested breathing moved closer. What would these things look like? Would he actually recognize someone, or...

The stench was horrible. Wysinski opened his eyes. He saw the dregs of emergency light glowing faintly through yellow plastic fixtures along the tunnel walls, but mainly there were deep shadows. And a figure approaching, backlit, a hulking outline, at once solid and darkly translucent...two indistinct layers. Inside was a face imbedded in a thick gelatinous substance of oily green. The face. It came closer. No, it was *not* human. The face was gone: What remained were yellowed eyes, the holes for mouth and nose...teeth, no lips.

It stopped. Hovered. Stank.

A bulbous, dripping paw—a giant slug reached out almost languidly.

Wysinski closed his eyes once more. His hand fumbled for his holster. He prayed.

"Now I lay me down to sleep, I pray the Lord my soul to keep. If I should die..."

It caressed his face.

CHAPTER ONE

The little white church sat like a wooden toy on the perimeter
of the university grounds, its steeple bell ringing joyfully.
"Rejoice! Rejoice!" the bell seemed to say.

And the day was alive with the fragrance of wisteria, magnolia and palmetto blossoms. A hot noon with butterflies and
the fuzz-buzzing of small insects. A large dog barking somewhere, sheep bleating. A place that seemed all at once too
close, then too far away because the air had that peculiar
translucency that only old plantations wear.

No people to see, not yet. Just the setting for a Norman
Rockwell canvas, some old buildings, some not so old, some
dating back to the Civil War, though. Everything laid out in
casual precision. General Oglethorpe, the architect of Savannah, Georgia, would have liked the arrangement: the large oval
roadway that encircled a grassy mall; the colonnaded houses
that had been private homes, then classrooms, and were now
something else; graceful wooden columns, Doric, Ionic and
Corinthian, paint peeling; green shutters hanging askew; the
grass in the mall, a little too high for comfortable sitting or
reading; the impressive gymnasium at the top of the road, at
the far end; the fairly modern two-story brick buildings with

15

ivy clutching at cracked textures; a row of plain columned group dwellings, not dormitories but rooms side by side, connected by an old brick walkway and covered by a slate roof—an architectural steal from Thomas Jefferson's University of Virginia.

In front of the largest manor house lay a vegetable garden where a fine lawn used to be. Behind the garden, a bronze statue of Robert E. Lee. General Lee's uppermost parts were stained white from pigeons perched on his illustrious head.

Then, gradually, as the church bell stopped ringing, another sound was heard. The soft purr of an engine. Then a moving red dot appeared and disappeared between trees and buildings, traveling along the circular roadway.

Two young men rode the red motorcycle with red jeep gas cans strapped like saddlebags on both sides of the rear fenders. On closer look the bike seemed to burp rather than purr. Driving was nineteen-year-old Billy Bob Morris, who wore a forty-dollar cowboy Stetson over his long, blond curls. A meaty fellow, a weight-lifter type, muscles bulging through a pale green T-shirt that said "survivor" in black, faded letters. Both boys wore patched Levi's.

"Beer! Did ya get the beer?" yelled Billy Bob over the engine.

Sonny Vandergot, seventeen, the more sensibly proportioned of the two and riding pillion, smiled.

"Was the Pope Polish?" Could be the last six-pack of Budweiser in Georgia. He adjusted the yellow strap on his right shoulder. The nylon pack was huge and chock full of goodies for the trip.

The trail bike slowed at the entrance to the university grounds. The main road lay ahead, its black surface severely cracked, strewn with five years of debris. Potholes within potholes. Extraordinary weeds and flowers climbed through chunks of dry, molting tar.

"Doesn't anybody pay taxes?" cried Sonny. Billy Bob gunned the bike east, belting Stephen Foster at the top of his well-exercised lungs.

"Camptown races five miles long, doo-dah! Doo-dah! Camptown races five miles long, oh, da doo-dah day!"

The sounds of a summer day in the old South! Mellow, fragrant sounds that somehow went with the picture. That fit.

The clink of hammer against metal. The village smithy? Yes, that fit, but the large horse poking his head through an open classroom window decidedly did not. A young pink-eyed palomino was staring out of J. Claudius Stern's old classroom.

In this very spot, to standing room only. J.C. had made American history come alive for even the most diffident Harding College student. He'd been a brilliant professor who researched his material so carefully that you never confused warts with beauty marks. You believed this kind of history.

But now the room contained only a horse, a shirtless black man and a German shepherd. The student desk chairs, still screwed to the oak floor, sat in even rows like gravestones—wooden gravestones with names scrawled on top. And petrified chewing gum stuck beneath in memoriam.

The young man was Nathan Delano Jones—rawboned with sinuous forearms and powerful back. He sat on a wooden stool with the foot of the palomino curled across his knee and drove small angular nails into the shiny metal horseshoe. Then a fly bit the horse's flank. The hoof jerked and hammer collided with thumbnail.

"Damn you, Arafat, stand still!" cried Nathan.

Max, another survivor lying under the blackboard, wagged his tail quickly, further agitating the giant horsefly, which was now sniping at his rectum. Max, the dog. Nathan, his master. Whenever Nathan cursed, Max raised his eyebrows as if to say, "Why me?"

Why me, boss? Max was two years old, the only surviving pup from his litter. His prospective brothers and sisters had been born dead or deformed. His mother had died soon after the birth. His father had been eaten by a marauding alligator from the nearby swamp. Max had had one carnal fling with that trashy collie named Scarlett who tended the sheep, but no pregnancy had resulted from this union.

Nathan dropped Arafat's hoof to the floor. And standing, he brushed the horse gently all the way down to its rump, where a cancerous lesion had again developed. Flies kept the wound open, promoted infection. The horse would need penicillin and additional antirad shots soon.

"More difficult keeping you alive than us," Nathan said to himself.

Antirad shots were painful. Your arm ached for hours, but they were mandatory once a week. They were no cure, but they kept the strontium 90 in your bone marrow temporarily at bay. Once a week or your life. If you disdained treatment, you simply died from vomiting and defecating within two weeks.

Yes, Nathan had watched them die. The old and the young. The inoculated and the uninoculated. The shots didn't help everyone. His own Elizabeth had succumbed while six months pregnant with their child. Of the forty-odd people inoculated a week before the war, fifteen were left. He had been very much in love with Liz. She was an islander too. From Daufuskie, just off the coast of South Carolina—an island populated entirely by black shrimpers, fishermen and their families.

His father had made casting nets. Not of nylon like the new delicate Japanese models, but of tough twisted cotton with bone sleeve. The Jones family had handmade their casting nets for shrimpers ever since Reconstruction days, when a small plot of the old Daufuskie plantation had been deeded to his great-great-grandfather. The nets were designed not to tangle and not to tear, but the Japanese kind were much less expensive. It took time to handcraft a good, solid net for each order. And time had become as expensive as everything else.

Nathan had gone to grade school in Beaufort, South Carolina. He and others, including Liz, had been boated every Monday to the mainland, and boated back to Daufuskie each Friday. They stayed weekdays with "adoptive parent groups" paid by the state government to take them in. The new generation would not be illiterate.

Nathan snapped the nylon tie to Arafat's bridle and led him from the classroom. Down the dark hallway they walked, the horse's newly shod hooves clapping echoes against the scarred linoleum.

When he listened carefully, Nathan thought he could hear students' voices. "Ghosts," he whispered. "Just ghosts."

If heaven were a large condominium, as Liz once guessed, then how difficult it must have been putting up all those people. Ghosts were people in between with no place to stay, weren't they? How God-awful lonely they must be, thought Nathan.

He pushed open the double door at the end of the corridor and led his horse and dog out into the hot, early-morning sun.

Chintz curtains flicked softly at the rusted Big Ben alarm on Dr. Frank Alden's bedside table. Beside the alarm stood a kerosene lamp, glasses and a green medical book titled *Obstetrics,* by C. J. Malone, M.D.

Frank snored. Except for a semiflattened nose from high-school boxing days, his features were regular and moderately well designed, framed as they were against a flowered pillow slip. His beard was graying with splotches of red and dark brown. His high forehead and thinning hair lent his sleeping countenance a natural intelligence.

Snip, snap went the curtains.

Frank's eyelid trembled, then opened tentatively as if asking a question. For a moment he stared at the brown plaster crumbling from the antebellum ceiling. He yawned. He looked at the alarm clock.

Eight thirty-three. But his first appointment was at nine. Mustn't be late again. Waking up early Sunday was depressing.

As a child he'd always slept late on holidays, and the habit had stuck.

The back of his wife's blond head poked up through the print sheet; the sweet scent of her body caught his nostrils. Been a month since they'd made love. Frank scowled. He looked over his head and into the bars of the tarnished brass bedstead. A stethoscope hung there. He removed it and plugged it to his ears. He pushed himself into a semisitting position and spoke quietly into the funnel end.

"Testing, one, two, three. It is Easter Sunday morning, April 3, 1988 . . . honey . . . ?"

"Mmmm . . . ?"

"Time to get up."

"Mmmmm . . ."

With his right hand Frank peeled down the flowered sheet to reveal his beautiful wife in her favorite pink cotton nightie. How many times had he undone those shiny little buttons and kissed the triangular arrangement of moles just below the nape of her neck? How many times had he slipped this garment over her head and touched his lips to her warm, rounded breasts? How many times? And each time was just like the first. How could that be? Frank was, by his own definition, a hopeless romantic.

Slowly he pulled the pink hem above Anita's waist and stared at her contoured whiteness. Sighing, he looped the stethoscope across her bare waist and planted its stainless-steel tip against her unseen stomach.

"Um . . . cold, Frank . . . cold, honey." Anita raised her knees up into the fetal position.

Frank leaned over her, still listening, kissing the moles and working his way down her tapered back.

19

"Ummmm... warm... getting warmer."

"Big day ahead, time to rise," he whispered gently. He turned her over.

"Really... mmmm..."

"Really," he answered. He removed the stethoscope and put it back over the bedstead.

"God," said Anita; she yawned and threw her arms around him. "Shots, hmm?" Her eyes were still closed.

"Umm," said Frank, his groin aching. "Up we go." Gradually he pulled away from her relaxed embrace and tweaked the belly button protruding from her nine-month-pregnant abdomen. Frank felt dizzy as he stood.

"Sermon ready?" asked Anita. Her eyes opened; they were vibrant green.

"What's left of it." Frank stumbled blearily into the bathroom and turned on the cold water. The old pipes rumbled.

"But you're still worried?"

"About my sermon?" he said, taking off his pajama top.

"About Randolph."

Frank squirted half an inch of Crest toothpaste onto a blue soft-bristled brush. "Sometimes I feel like Dr. Frankenstein. What if my monster gets up to speak for the first time, then wets his pants?"

Anita stretched languidly up from the bed. "Frank, that's not very charitable. I like Randolph."

"I do too."

Someone knocked at the door of their one-and-a-half-room ground-floor apartment.

"Who is it?" asked Anita, rising.

"Eric, ma'am," said the young voice beyond the door. "Is Doc up yet?"

Anita reached for her bathrobe. "Just a minute, Eric."

She opened the door.

"Everyone's waiting at the hospital, again," said Eric. He was fifteen, with blond, curly hair and speckled gray eyes. A faded Darth Vader with brandished sword emblazoned his T-shirt.

Frank poked his head around the bathroom doorjamb.

"What'd you say, Eric?" Frank could see Eric's slightly superior smile. Eric was his assistant—a good one who wanted to be a scientist—dedicated, inspired, very alert, but he had that smirk that curled up one side of his cherubic mouth. "I don't have the key to let them in," said Eric.

"What do you mean? What time is it?" asked Frank, his voice rising. Oh, God, that damn rusting piece of junk, he thought and made for the Big Ben on the bedside table. He snatched it up, put it to his ear, cursed.

"Sorry, Eric, gimme a second. . . ." Frank shifted into high gear as he moved toward the dresser. "The keys . . . Christ . . . where are the keys?"

As usual he pushed things around, obscuring a lot and finding nothing. He opened the closet, stuffed his hands into various jacket pockets, getting angrier each second.

"Frank . . . ?"

Frank turned to his wife. She held a huge ring of keys between her thumb and forefinger, as if she had just pulled them from a magician's top hat.

Anita tossed the keys to Eric. Frank grinned sheepishly. "You start, Eric, I'm right behind you!"

Eric's smirk widened to an open smile; to Anita, not to Frank. "Thanks!" he said, turned immediately and started walking out from under the colonnade and onto the grass that blanketed the mall. Across the mall he could see eight people in front of a two-story ivied brick building. Nathan's palomino grazed beside a small walnut tree. Eric waved the keys over his head.

Frank jumped into his sweat clothes and quickly tied on his running shoes. He'd been late twice in one month. Big Ben would have to go. He threw open the door and slammed it behind him. That's right, blame it on the damned alarm clock, you spoiled, upper-middle-class bastard! Eric was walking swiftly across the mall. He looked over his shoulder as Frank ran toward him, then took off running himself. Obviously he wanted to race. Frank obliged. Frank kicked out, and stretching his long legs, gained quickly on the boy. The runners skirted the vegetable garden close to a flapping scarecrow; were neck-and-neck as they passed Robert E. Lee, standing with bronze hat in hand, three pigeons on his white head. The pigeons fluttered into the sky.

Frank opened the hospital door, let everyone in. The group proceeded down the hall to the emergency room, rolled up their sleeves, stood in line. Luckily, the solution had been prepared the night before, the injector gun was ready. Eric had seen to those details. Eric stood beside Frank with cotton swabs soaked in alcohol.

21

Velma Lee Jenkins was first. She wore no makeup, her clothes were colorful and handmade—a crocheted cotton tank top and skirt for Easter Sunday. She was fourteen, tall and skinny, with steel-rim glasses.

Frank pulled the trigger of the gun. It clicked, and 2.5 cc's of a super protein fluid was injected intramuscularly into Velma's arm.

"Ouch . . . I hate that. Why don't we go back to needles?"

"This is faster," said Frank, smiling. "I have to practice my marksmanship, and besides, we're running out of needles."

"I hate it," said Velma, rubbing her arm. She took a few steps, then dropped to her hands and did ten regulation push-ups. "Helps the circulation," said Velma over her shoulder as her adopted brother Henry moved to the front of the line.

"Hi, Henry," said Frank. Henry didn't talk much. He nodded, eyes darting from side to side. He was eleven, with a sad little angelic face. His mother and father and two older brothers had all died of radiation poisoning four and a half years ago. For whatever reason, thought Frank, Henry's serum had taken perfectly. Henry stared at the gun as it touched his arm. His attempt at a brave smile withered.

Click. Henry ducked his head so that Frank could not see his pain and moved away quickly. Frank watched him go. He was always keenly aware of people's reactions to injections. Long-repressed fears were often revealed at this moment of truth.

Lynne Jenkins, Velma's mother, was next. "How's Anita?" she asked. She wore a near-translucent Indian cotton shirt and tight cord skirt with a madras belt.

"She's fine, Lynne." Lynne had nearly died from her last miscarriage. Frank felt pity for her. Her eyes were very blue and sexy, but just this side of hysterical. Frank always looked at people's eyes. They mirrored not only the soul, but also people's mental and physical health.

"Frank, you're a born sadist. I kinda like it." The blue eyes blinked in pain as the shot hit home. The red mouth smiled as if to say, I'm just kidding with the sexual innuendo. Frank knew better. Since the war, Lynne, like many others, had become obsessed with sex. To Frank's mind this was natural. Under present conditions he couldn't fault anyone's desperate need to procreate.

Lynne's husband stepped forward.

Roy Jenkins was a tall, rumpled, good-looking man at fifty,

who wore a thin moustache. Frank enjoyed his Okie accent and friendly manner. Roy also was a good physics teacher. His only weakness was alcohol.

"Your stuff makes me constipated," complained Roy. "By the time I get the old pipes clean, it's Sunday again."

"Keeps you goin', Roy." Frank fired the gun. He could smell wine on the man's breath. "How 'bout a laxative?"

"No, thank you, bud," he said, patting Frank on the shoulder, "too many grim reminders."

Frank saw Nathan move forward—big, black Nathan, who could have played for any college football team in the country if he'd ever finished high school.

"Need more serum for Arafat, Doc," said Nathan. Frank pulled the trigger. Suddenly there was blood on Nathan's arm. Eric handed Nathan a wad of wet cotton and he pressed it to the tiny wound. "Let me know if that doesn't stop bleeding in a few minutes," said Frank. He turned to look out of the hospital window at Nathan's grazing horse.

In the early 1920s this building had been a private mental clinic. The curved bars disturbed him.

"What's wrong with him now?"

"Flies keep after the sore. It won't heal."

"Get a move on up there," said Wilkes Bonner. Nathan turned and gave Bonner a quick, hard look. Frank knew Nathan didn't like Wilkes. Twice they'd fought.

"Hurry up and wait, huh?" said Wilkes, moving forward. He was a short, powerful man, nearly bald at forty-eight, an ex-professional soldier who'd had political run-ins with Frank during their Vietnam years at Harding College. Wilkes had been a staff NCO with the AROTC; weapons instruction was his specialty, "Bomb 'em back to the Stone Age," his motto. "Sorry to be late, Wilkes," said Frank. "I'd make a lousy soldier." Wilkes nodded, not friendly, not particularly unfriendly, just in agreement. Frank squeezed the trigger. The shot smacked in just below the rolled sleeve of Wilkes's faded khaki shirt, where master sergeant stripes had once been attached. "Damn, you're gettin' pretty good with that thing," said Wilkes.

Nancy Jean Jefferies, a voluptuous seventeen wearing a size small T-shirt over a size C bosom, stood fetchingly in Wilkes's vacated spot. Her T-shirt read, "I'M WITH STUPID." A printed thumb pointed accusingly.

Nancy grinned and thumbed back to Kirk Cosgrove, his

hands thrust deep into his Levi's pockets. "Kirk's got something important to tell you, Doc." Frank fired quickly, catching her off guard.

"What's that, Kirk?" Nancy walked away pumping her arm up and down. She kept a wary eye on Kirk, who shifted weight from one leg to the other, obviously very uncomfortable.

"We were gonna get married this Sunday, but there's too much goin' on," said Kirk, avoiding Nancy's gaze. "Maybe next weekend, huh?"

Kirk had been put up to this. "Let's talk about it first," said Frank.

"Don't worry," said Kirk.

"Marriage is something you don't enter into lightly, the responsibilities are . . ."

". . . maybe more than I can handle," whispered Kirk, his head turned away from Nancy.

"I see. . . ." said Frank. He knew that Nancy had tried to marry Sonny, then Billy. Now Kirk.

"I love her, though," admitted Kirk reluctantly. "I'm really torn."

"We'll all three talk later, okay?"

"Okay," said Kirk. "Thanks, Doc." Kirk ambled away, almost a reincarnation of his father with his crew cut and short, slim, muscular frame. Frank used to spar with Ken, who had headed up the physical education department at Harding.

Left alone now to their weekly routine, Frank pressed the gun to Eric's arm. Eric flinched.

"Get it?" asked Frank, grinning.

"Got it," said Eric. He took the gun and turned it on Frank.

"Good," said Frank with a grunt; his arm was already hot and swelling.

"Billy and Sonny?" asked Frank, for the first time realizing they were absent.

"Don't know," said Eric, preparing to clean the injector gun. "I heard their bike early this morning."

"Yeah?" said Frank, shivering.

"You want me to take care of Nathan's horse?" asked Eric.

"If you would."

"Sure," said Eric. "I'd also like to run that film again later this morning if you don't mind."

"As long as you can talk Anita out of kitchen duty. You'll pay later."

"Don't worry."

"Eric?"

"Yes, sir?"

"Unwind a little bit. You've gotten very tense lately." Frank shivered again, but this time it was more of a shudder.

"You okay?" asked Eric, looking up from the gun. "Get a reaction to the shot?"

"No," said Frank, smiling through his discomfort. "Like my Irish mother used to say, someone just walked over my grave."

The Yamaha cruised down an empty country road. Pine trees flashed by as the dirt bike zigzagged across the faded white line, avoiding an extraordinary number of potholes.

Billy could smell the ocean now. It was a smell that made him feel strong, glad to be alive. Sitting on a beach, swimming, and especially lifting weights always made Billy feel strong; made him feel more in control of his life, of his feelings, more able to cope with the terrible sense of isolation that gripped his soul some nights, keeping him awake till daybreak. Sex helped too. When very insecure, he masturbated, sometimes twice a night.

Sonny tapped Billy's shoulder, pointed up ahead. Water. They were approaching a section of the Inland Waterway.

CHAPTER TWO

It was 10:00 A.M.

Kirk and Nancy ran down the sidewalk toward the Cosgrove Memorial Gymnasium, Kirk dribbling a basketball, Nancy frantically trying to take it away from him but getting more and more frustrated by the moment.

"Gimme the ball, Kirk, give it to me, you... you little shrimp!"

Kirk Cosgrove was an inch and a half shorter than Nancy Jean Jefferies—a difference she never let him forget.

Nancy lunged for the ball and missed again. "I'll stomp your foot next time!"

Nancy swung the gym door open. Kirk feinted a shot over her head but fired the ball instead through her well-shaped legs. They both ran after it, but Kirk was there first and booted it up through the metal rafters, sending sparrows flying from their nests.

The gym was full of so many "odd" things: bales of hay stacked against the walls, a couple of farm tractors, a large yellow oil tank marked *"Gasoline*, DO NOT TOUCH!," sacks of grain, seeds, fertilizer and a wire pen full of young and old chickens, clucking. Obviously this was a working barn.

The only grudging nod toward gymnastics was an Olympic-sized trampoline and pommel horse—its leather dark from oil and sweat.

Kirk's small eyes fairly jittered with excitement. He ran to the other end of the gym and leaped up onto the handles of the pommel horse. Then, with muscles flexing, he began a fast series of twists and turns that propelled his body almost effortlessly in graceful arcs above and around the horse.

Nancy watched her spinning, twisting hero with almost morbid fascination. How could anyone be that graceful? "Kirk, you could have been a movie star! Didn't they used to make Hollywood actors stand on boxes to look taller? You could have done that!" She tried to visualize Kirk on a wooden box on tiptoes French-kissing Olivia Newton-John. Then she frowned jealously at the scene she'd fashioned, and said to herself, "Why, that lady's old enough to be his mother!"

"What?" said Kirk, as he completed one final swing and dropped to the urethaned floor with a flourish.

"Nothing!" she said.

Kirk laughed. He skipped over to the trampoline, and with no motion wasted, began to spring higher and higher with manic intensity. On the last bounce he did a two-and-a-half somersault, and landing facedown on the woven nylon, vaulted nimbly to his feet. Kirk was hardly perspiring as he reached his hand down for Nancy.

"Up we go!"

Nancy grabbed him by the wrist and he yanked her up beside him. At first they bounced seesaw style, grinning like two kids on the playground.

A while later, in the dim, cavernous cement room beneath the gym, Kirk and Nancy took a shower together. Pulsing water massaged her back, and Nancy, raising both her long legs to straddle her boyfriend's hips, felt his powerful hands grip her buttocks.

"Sometimes my being a little taller has certain advantages, doesn't it, Kirk?" she whispered greedily. Her eyes were half closed, her cheek rubbing against Kirk's forehead. "Next weekend, Kirk . . . next weekend."

Obviously they were unafraid of anyone coming downstairs to disturb them.

Across the campus an organ was playing.

On the clapboard exterior beside the open church doors a small wooden plaque recently had been erected. It read: THE VANDERGOT CHAPEL.

Inside, Anita Alden was coaching a choir of four. The organ she was playing faced the choir stalls, the choir members not fully dressed yet for the Sunday afternoon "anniversary service." The church, a quite beautiful one, was decorated simple Low Episcopalian, and the graceful ceiling made of old pine resembled the wide belly of a large overturned ark.

The singers were Henry Baldwin, Velma Lee Jenkins and Mr. and Mrs. Jenkins. They were singing in perfect harmony.

A Big Ben alarm went off suddenly somewhere in the church. Anita stopped playing in midphrase. Vibrations from the frantic clapper jiggled the clock from its tenuous perch in the nave and it fell with a smash to the floor.

"Henry!" exclaimed Anita. The boy winced.

Roy Jenkins's long arm grabbed Henry by the collar. "Damn-it, Henry!" His voice was angry and nasal. "One more trick like that one, buddy, an' I'll tan your little hide!"

Lynne Jenkins immediately came to the rescue. There was an obvious textbook difference in her chosen method of applying the punishment to the crime. She kneeled down beside Henry and talked to him as an equal. Henry nodded and looked as though he might cry. Finally, Lynne kissed the boy on his cheek and stood.

Henry smiled through craftily manufactured tears and mumbled something like being sorry. Then, as the organ began once more, he stared up at Jesus in the stained-glass window closest to him. Christ was writhing in pain on his crude wooden cross. No offense, Henry thought. No offense, okay?

But Henry knew exactly what time the second alarm clock would ring during the afternoon sermon. He just couldn't help it.

CHAPTER THREE

The old Vandergot house was handsome clapboard Greek Revival with fourteen Doric columns around the front and the sides. Fairly well kept, it sat on a fraction of its original fine lawn. It had once been planted with beautiful shrubbery and huge magnolia trees. Built in 1835 by a General Harrison Lamar, who surrounded it with wood gardens and built many greenhouses, the original plan specified only four columns. But as the building progressed, the number grew. The general often was heard to chuckle and say, "Got to sell another slave; my wife wants four more columns."

The house had served as a Confederate hospital during the Civil War. Afterward, it and other nearby buildings became the bases for a small Georgia preparatory school specializing in agriculture. A hundred sixty acres of this and surrounding property were purchased by the Vandergot family of Boston in 1905 as a private nursing home and mental asylum for the elderly well-to-do.

Mimi Vandergot had lived in this house for the past forty-one years. She was a striking old woman—tall, thin, with a long, prominent nose that dispelled any doubts about her lineage. She was Anglo-Saxon with a hint of French Huguenot about the eyes. Dressed in a Japanese silk robe, she used her left hand to open an antique glass kitchen cabinet. Her ring finger sparkled with a huge engagement stone and diamond band. She pulled on the silver knob, opened the door and removed a tin box of Earl Grey tea. She set down the box on the Formica counter of her modern kitchen—modern except for the wood-burning stove which stuck out awkwardly at the center of the room. The contents of a teapot boiled. She looked at her watch. It was eleven o'clock.

Someone cried out from the next room, "DON'T! OH, GOD, NO!"

"Randolph!" said Mimi as she went through the swinging door into the dining room.

She walked quickly past the elegant dark mahogany table and chairs with their lion-clawed feet, past the matching sideboard and into the living room, where an old Persian carpet began.

Her son Randolph sat slumped in his wheelchair in the penumbral shadow of the bright front windows. His hands clawed at his face; a pillow lay askew behind his head. "No . . . nooo . . ." he cried pitifully.

Mimi knelt in front of him. She took his wrists and removed his hands. Exactly half the man's face was a hideous pink rubbery scar—a keloid tumor from nuclear flash burn.

"Another dream?" ventured Mimi quietly.

Randolph nodded as his mind returned slowly to the present, his eyes glazed with tears. "We're . . . you and I are taking communion . . . the devil's there . . . wearing a soft mask . . ."

"A mask?"

"Of Sonny, he looked like my son."

Mimi kissed his forehead, then hugged him like a young child. Her southern voice soft and tranquil. "Now, there . . . now, now . . . don't be afraid, Randolph. Hush . . ."

She looked at him sadly and wiped tears from his cheek.

He, Randolph, had been their only progeny, and she and Ben had agreed to spoil him right from the beginning. Because he was such a bright child, it had been manifestly impossible to punish him. Why, from age two on they were able to reason with the boy. He was toilet trained at one and a half. Now, at forty-seven, he was their U.S. senator from Georgia, elected for a second term.

Mimi tried to let her natural strength flow into her son's body. He definitely was improving. For nearly five years he

32

had been as silent as death. Dr. Frank Alden, who had taken over her husband's good works at the university, had said that Randolph was suffering from "total abject shock." "Aren't we all," she had murmured. But when Randolph finally did speak to her last month, his remembrance of the holocaust in Washington, D.C., after the missiles fell rivaled anything she had read about Hiroshima or Nagasaki. Compared to the rest of the country, especially big cities, we've had it easy, she thought. She did, however, recall vividly the day a Russian missile exploded on the northeast edge of the Okefenokee, about thirty miles away. First there was a flash, then a few seconds later an incredible blast of ruptured air. Oddly, there was no sound, only the familiar mushroom cloud. And instant darkness, as the heavy-laden clouds made twilight of the afternoon sun.

They had been lucky the wind was blowing from the southwest. If it had blown in the opposite direction, they might not have been here today no matter how many of Ben's special protein shots they'd received. If there were devils afoot this day and age, they would be the devils of a technology gone so berserk it literally destroyed itself, not the terrible slimy monsters that Randolph dreamed of.

"They're dreams, Randolph, just dreams," she said. She was sure of that.

"There were maggots in his hands, Mama..."

"There, there...now, now..." said Mimi again. "You've been reading too much of that Old Testament stuff; you can't take it literally..."

Randolph closed his eyes once more, this time caressing his mother's wrinkled hands. "You have such nice hands, Mama..."

"Perk up now," said Mimi, standing. "You've got to speak for your father today. No one realizes how much progress you've made the past few months."

"Except Dr. Alden..." said Randolph with a rumpled smiled.

On cue, Frank approached the foot of the front porch stairs. He was now wearing chinos and a denim shirt and carrying his black leather doctor's bag. "Hello!" he called.

Seconds later Mimi appeared at the front doot. "Hi, Frank. Come on in."

Frank ran up the stairs and kissed Mimi on both of her cheeks. "How's my second-best girl feeling?"

Mimi grinned. "Which end do you want me to start with? Come on in."

As they entered the hallway, Randolph spun his wheelchair to face them.

"You all set for today?" asked Frank.

"Piece-a-cake," answered Randolph.

"Remember, Senator," said Frank lightly, "you're not trying to get votes. Just be yourself."

"Whoever that is," said Randolph, smiling despite his spastic face. "Shall I roll up my sleeve?"

"You remembered," said Frank, smiling back. "Good man; that's two weeks in a row now." Frank dug immediately into his bag and brought out two packaged syringes and vials. "Well, let's get it over with till next week."

Mimi did a quick nervous take and headed for the kitchen. Frank laughed and called after her. "Come on back here, Mimi. You can thank your brilliant husband for this."

But Mimi already had escaped. She opened the tin and said over her thin shoulder, "Would you like some tea, Doctor? I have the last can of Earl Grey in Georgia."

Frank winked conspiratorially to Randolph. "That's an offer I cannot refuse, ma'am!"

Henry rode the church bell rope up and down. Up and down went Henry. Up and down.

Busy hands were at work in the large stainless-steel church kitchen. Everyone wore aprons. Nancy Jean stirred her garlic-laden spaghetti sauce, bubbling on the wood stove. Anita diced vegetables. Velma prepared the peaches while her mother flattened out yards of whole-wheat pie dough with a huge wooden rolling pin.

"Eleven after eleven," said Lynne, glancing at her ladies' Rolex. "What's the bell for now?"

Velma shrugged. "Probably Henry again. He's bats about bells."

"Very funny," said her mother.

"You let the little creep get away with murder, Mother."

Velma threw up her hands. "Maybe it's the full moon, or something. You know what Henry did last night? He collected about five thousand daddy longlegs from beneath the house and put them under my bed covers."

"Oh, God," exclaimed Lynne. She hated spiders of any kind.

"I sleep nude, Mom," continued Velma. "When I got in the bed it was the most horrible thing I've ever felt. They were all

34

over me . . . and you know what those things smell like when you squish them, they . . ."

"That's enough, Velma . . ."

Velma sighed. "It's everything I can do each day now not to strangle . . ."

"Henry's a case, Velma . . . we have to . . ."

"I know he's an orphan," said Velma angrily, "but he's using that. He's using it, Mom."

Velma dumped too much brown sugar into the pie filling, controlled her growing rage and proceeded to take most of it out again.

The portable Honda generator was throbbing exhaust into the hospital hallway as Frank opened the door to his laboratory/classroom. Inside, blackout shades were down, and light from a sixteen-millimeter projector poured onto a small screen attached to the top of the chalkboard. Eric, the only person in the room, sat beside the projector as a basso announcer's voice droned over a lovely travelog-type beach.

Frank slipped into a seat in the back row. The film Eric had chosen to see for the fifth time was called *Mondo Cane*—Italian, and made at least twenty years ago. As Frank watched, he wondered how many films had ever been done on the genetic defects of animals surviving atomic tests. Why hadn't more information on this subject been released from government classified data to the public? Had most of the Italian film crew shooting the film died of cancer years later? Had they conceived healthy children? Not that all this speculation mattered; everyone would be dead now.

But he watched the film with growing anxiety.

A giant mother sea turtle ready to lay her eggs lumbered from the gentle surf onto the beach. "But her eggs are sterile from radiation in the surrounding ocean," said the announcer. Whereupon there was a cut to the turtle having just laid her eggs. She arose slowly and looked around in bewilderment.

"It should be a natural thing for her to return to the sea. But . . . her instincts have been altered, and instead she blunders over the nearest dune."

The image of the turtle crossing the sand faded out. A different image faded in: A brutal noonday sun revealed hundreds of dead mother sea turtles, skin dried, their bones already baking and bleaching through. The sandy interior of the island stripped of all vegetation was wall-to-wall tortoise-shell.

Then another victim of the atomic test blast on Bikini atoll was shown and described by the narrator: A small tropical fish walked from the edge of the sea, hobbling across the hot sand on its pectoral fins, as if on crutches. It then began to burrow like a snake.

A few years and many generations of fish later, the camera zoomed up into a palm tree. A now distant relative to the first fish was actually hiding within the tree's leafy fronds. Its mouth more beaklike; its tail, much less defined.

Then, in a clinical laboratory shot of the dead "fish," a scalpel pointed to the pectoral fins, which were now becoming residual wings. There also was a bulging indication that a pair of fins closer to the tail were becoming something like legs.

"In one way presenting a pathetic commentary on man's technological advances...in another, the miracle of nature's uncanny adaptability to endure and survive," the announcer said. When the subject matter changed to Ceylonese fakirs being hung by the skin of their back from many small fishhooks, Eric turned off the projector and went to the back of the room. He flipped up the blackout shades at each large window and sunlight streamed in. Piercing blue skies shined brightly on Eric's intelligent fifteen-year-old face.

Frank got up, stepped outside the door and killed the generator. When he returned, Eric leveled his first question at the teacher.

"Could you say that large changes in the physical construction of a creature don't necessarily require large changes in genetic structure?"

"You've been reading what's left of my mind, Eric," said Frank. "Yep, I'd say that heavy radiation really can spin the old evolutionary time clock."

"And our children," said Eric quickly. "Do you think our own children will suffer disabling mutations?"

Frank flinched. He preferred not to think about this. The boy suddenly was alarmed by his own question. He stuttered, "I'm...I'm sorry, I..."

"No problem," said Frank, coming to the rescue. "It's an important question, one we'll be asking ourselves for many years to come."

But Frank took his time answering. He walked slowly toward his desk at the front of the room. He could see his Plexiglas clipboard, the one given him by a former student. He walked up behind his desk, pulled the screen and let it flap back into its metal box. The title from yesterday's lesson, "DNA, Plasmid, Foreign Growth and Genetic Machinery," was instantly visible on the chalkboard.

"Wouldn't be the first time in our evolution we have changed to compensate for environment," he said slowly, like a fat man crossing a tightrope. "That we look and act like we do now is maybe a million-to-one shot."

A grim smile returned to Frank's lips. Teaching was one of life's curious joys, no matter how painful the subject. His jaw unclenched.

"Man, for instance, still carries residual gills just behind his jaw," he continued. "At one time we were fishlike underwater breathers ourselves. Then, when tidal basins across the world began to thicken with primordial ooze and we had a hard time getting oxygen from the water—at some point, while strangling in that putrid water—we opted to get our oxygen from the air. So we probably wriggled out on our pectoral fins with the same specific intent to survive on land." He looked right at Eric, his words measured with a strong personal feeling. "However, it was a momentous decision made over millions of years. Extreme radioactivity, as you've just seen, would seem to speed up that whole process. But—and this is a very important 'but'—the key to change is finally knowing in our genes that we must survive at any cost. And the primary key to natural survival, or selection, is adaptation. Eventually either we adapt to our environment or die out as a species."

Eric looked at the ten fingers of his hands. "But we haven't adapted, have we?"

"No, not really," Frank answered. "We're marking time. We survive as long as we keep taking shots. We're lucky they're an easy prescription to fill, but they can't work forever. Mother Nature never favors those who try to preempt her. I'm just hoping that all our children will develop a *natural* immunity."

"Me too, Doc." Eric nodded sympathetically.

"Thanks . . ." Frank glanced at his clipboard. "To Dr. Alden for inspiration," read the engraved inscription. It was signed, "Mitch." "See you at the anniversary service," said Frank after a moment of thought. "Everyone may be lucky today, Eric; I have a very short sermon prepared."

When Eric had left, Frank erased the chalkboard and thought

of the baby in his wife's womb. It was a strange world to bring a child into. He and Anita had discussed the subject many times over the past four years. She had wanted a baby. He hadn't. Secretly, he was too depressed to attempt to raise a child. He had resisted strongly. But now that things were starting to even out for them... wasn't that what he'd told her? When things start to even out, maybe then. Always a maybe. Well, Anita simply took matters into her own expert hands and got pregnant. Frank knew that others had tried desperately and failed. It always was a difficult thing to talk about. The idea of becoming barren or sterile from the very air you breathed was totally repugnant to his nature. If man was stupid enough to destroy his own reproductive capability, then damnit, he didn't deserve to be around. Frank scowled. Why am I always trying to put the ball in someone else's court? *We* are *man*. We are and have been a part of man. Now we are an even smaller part. In three years there has been no communication with another community. As far as I know, we are "it," the "chosen" few.

And as far as his baby was concerned, Frank could do no more than wait to see if it had three eyes and a monster head. And then decide what to do with it. If the baby were not perfect, he knew Anita would not have the heart to try for another. Frank looked down at his moving hand and smiled bitterly.

His outline of words on the chalkboard had long since disappeared, but he still was pushing the eraser up and down. Here I am, one of fifteen people left on earth, teaching a course in biochemistry in what used to be an insane asylum.

"Yep. Must be a certain irony in that," he said aloud.

CHAPTER FOUR

The motorcycle had cruised southeast along Route 94, plunging down between Florida's Pinhook and Moccasin swamps, then across the very southern tip of Georgia (and into Florida), where 94 intersects with Interstate 95, heading north. The final objective was Crow's Nest Island near Jekyll Island. Sonny hoped the bridge still would span the Inland Waterway.

An awesome overabundance surrounded them. Within six months of the war the effect of radiation on the underground organs of plants had been extraordinary—an eruption of verdant green everywhere. A mysterious new Garden of Eden— a sunflower twenty feet high, a pecan tree strangled by wild fecund honeysuckle, blackberries as big as your fist. Technology's miraculous fertilizer had worked wonders on the billions of mutated bacteria in each handful of dark, swampy earth.

They had turned east from 95 now and they stopped just before crossing a rusting steel bridge.

"We used to come here when I was a kid!" Sonny yelled.

Billy Bob looked straight down the bridge road. "You think it's safe to cross?"

"Sure . . . no military installations in this area. Just the sand, the sun and the sea . . . and a six-pack! Let's do it!"

Billy Bob nodded. Sonny always "suggested" orders and Billy usually went along with the program. Sometimes, of course, he would resist when he didn't want to be taken for granted. His father, an odd-jobber, had been owner of a Mobil station in Waycross, then general handyman and gardener for the Vandergot family, so Billy practically had grown up with Sonny. Not, however, in the sense that they went to the same parties and social functions together. The Vandergots were "old family" rich. Not only did they have the largest tobacco field in the South, but they also had their son in the U.S. Senate. *Had* is right, Billy thought, poor guy's a vegetable now. Another story nobody talked about, especially Sonny, who had been the oldest kid in the family of five. Sonny had had the good luck to be visiting his grandparents during that Easter vacation from his Virginia prep school five years ago.

In Billy Bob's memory, the event, particularly about the airplane, was etched like a magical illustration from one of his boy's adventure books. He was just fourteen when the little Cessna landed in the field behind the gym. The adults tried to stop them but the kids went running outside to watch it anyway. Everybody was out there that day a few months after the war, wondering who it was. And the plane almost crashed. It just missed the cypress treetops in the swamp and didn't travel more than fifty feet before it hit a groundhog burrow and flipped over.

Billy Bob remembered the spastic crawling out of the plane—it was horrible; half his face was burned off and his bald-headed wife was crazy like a loon. Both the kids inside were dead, but the man pulled them out and laid them in the grass.

They had tried to help him but he wouldn't let anyone else touch his kids, not even Sonny, whom he didn't seem to recognize. Sonny's mother just screamed and cried. Later they found out she was blinded, eyeballs rotting in her sockets. A week later, when she died, all that man's hair turned perfectly white. Not a brown hair left on his whole head. That was truly amazing. Like some weird story you hear kids talk about over a campfire when you know it couldn't be true.

The grizzly etching faded and Billy heard the distant tumble of waves.

The motorcycle had crossed the bridge without incident. It

passed a dilapidated baitshop, a Calgo filling station, Roger's silver diner, the inelegant Sunrise Motel, then it turned right at a sandblasted stop sign that said absolutely nothing. The dunes had crept across the narrow beach road that led down the Atlantic coast into Crow's Nest Island.

Hundreds of years ago the island had acquired its name. Pirate ships used to hide behind the low dunes along the waterway side, their masts pulleyed close to the water and tied fast to stunted oak trees. When an unsuspecting merchant vessel passed through the channel, the lines were cut and the ships righted, ready to sail out and pounce on their prey.

Beach houses on either side of the duned road leaned precariously. A huge hurricane (which they'd named Adam) had passed through the area two years before. The closer the motorcycle got to the end of the island, the more evident Adam's destruction. Water had surged from a mountainous ocean across to the Inland Waterway, gobbling everything in its path. The entire southern end of the beach for maybe five miles was swept smoothly clean except for the odd foundation or piling.

The motorcycle chugged up a sand dune overpopulated with sea oats and stalked grass.

"Our beach house used to be right over there," said Sonny, gesturing vaguely to an empty area fronting the ocean.

He had hoped to explore the house, to look for childhood keepsakes: his red bamboo surfing rod, a handmade shrimp casting net, a special flounder gig for night fishing on the waterway shallows and especially the secondhand sailfish his father had bought him for his tenth birthday.

"Zilch," said Billy Bob respectfully. He could see his friend's disappointment.

At 1:25 P.M. they laid down the bike on the dune grass, stripped off their clothes and ran nude and screaming into the rolling waves. A new generation of sea gulls flying overhead circled the strange two-legged swimmers. A family of pelicans, resembling prehistoric pterodactyls, veered from their normal flight pattern over a school of small fish for a cautious flyover.

It was a perfect day. Nary a cloud in the burning blue sky. And the waves were a perfect height for body surfing.

That the beer was hot didn't matter. It went down like liquid gold. "The way they drink it in England," Sonny explained with a slight, patronizing grin. They were sitting on the sand at the water's edge.

"What makes you think there's still a friggin' England?"

41

asked Billy Bob, punching a hole in his second can and cutting his finger from so little practice. "Goddamn things were designed by some idiot!"

Sonny looked worried at the trickle of blood. "Better take care of that."

"Nah," Billy explained. "I had a cut last month and it healed right away. No sweat."

Sonny looked dubious. The problem was a slight bleeding tendency due to a higher-than-normal white-cell count. Shots alleviated but did not eliminate this tendency.

"Nobody's been catchin' fish around here for the past three or four years. Betcha there's some good-size speckled sea trout runnin'," said Sonny, changing the subject.

"They don't run till December. All you'd catch now would be mackerel."

"Maybe..." Sonny shrugged. Then he chugged the remainder of his second can, stood and pitched it out into the waves. "Just so those mackerel know that we're comin' back again." He looked behind him and shivered slightly. The cotton blanket was stretched out on the beach, the huge backpack sitting on one corner.

"It's gettin' cooler, huh? Play ya some ball?"

The protein serum in their bodies kept the afternoon's strong ultraviolet rays from cooking their skin. Neither boy had the slightest sunburn. They were still barefoot but wearing warmer clothes against the cool afternoon breeze. Their voices were hoarse from shouting over the crashing waves, which were much larger on the rising tide.

"Supposed to be a full moon tonight!" yelled Billy Bob.

"What?" asked Sonny, pitching the rubber football high into the sun. Billy Bob caught it over his head, forced it onto his belly and faded back for a pass. He looked around for imaginary opponents, stiff-armed one and hurled the ball to Sonny while running out of his quarterback's pocket to the right.

"I said, I think Kirk-the-Jerk's in love!"

"You are...?" Sonny caught the ball delicately with one hand.

"No, Kirk! Kirk! He's really in bad shape!"

"How?"

"Tried to punch me out yesterday!"

Sonny leaped high into the air, cocked his arm and threw. "Why?"

"I told him Nancy was lousy in bed!" said Billy Bob from a distance.

"That's true!"

Billy Bob grabbed the football on the run, bobbled it and then caught it again. "You still dig her?"

A pause. "She's okay!"

Billy Bob lay back and booted a high spiral. Sonny ran to get under it. Billy seemed angry and frustrated now.

"She said I was sterile! *STERILE*, MAN!"

"Maybe something's wrong with her!" commented Sonny with conviction.

He misjudged the high ball in the wind. It bounced off his chest and onto the sand. When he glanced up, Billy Bob really looked pathetic.

"I mean, we can't all three be sterile—no way, huh?"

"No way," Sonny agreed.

Billy Bob grinned nervously. "I mean, Doc Alden's thirty-nine years old and he came through..."

Sonny lateraled to Billy. "Yep, the doc's a real straight shooter!"

"Yeah," said Billy Bob, giggling, "but still it took him over four years! How 'bout Mrs. Jenkins?" Billy dropped back to throw. "I don't think she's married to old Jenkins. He's a boozer anyway!"

Sonny caught the ball. They both were breathing hard now. "What about her?"

"Oh, you know," said Billy Bob slyly, "she's been comin' on lately; you been with her?"

Sonny grinned wide with teenage lechery, curled the ball in his right arm and charged toward Billy Bob. "No sireee ...never touch the stuff, ole buddy!"

Billy Bob lowered his broad shoulders to tackle his friend, but Sonny spun off to his right. Billy grabbed a bare foot and managed to hold on. They both went down rolling on the sand, laughing. Billy came up spitting sand and persistent.

"Come on, Sonny...Mrs. Jenkins, sometimes she looks at you like..."

Billy Bob's gray eyes glazed over. He had this sudden steaming-hot visceral image. His mouth actually salivated.

"...like you were a Big Mac!"

"A Big Mac?" Sonny repeated, sputtering in surprised laughter.

"A Big Mac!" Billy said with even more emphasis, smacking his lips as a greasy aroma filled his nostrils. "Believe you me, I'd give up all my sex life for a Big Mac and a double chocolate shake!"

Billy Bob's voice dropped to a reverent whisper. "I even miss all those TV commercials . . . Pizza Hut, Jones Sausage, Oscar Meyer extra lean hot dogs . . . I mean, the food was there, man, the food was there! Now when you walk into your local supermarket all you see are thousands of deodorant sticks. Who the hell cares about BO?" Billy sniffed his own right armpit and did a comic pratfall as if passing out from the potency.

"My grandmother cares!" said Sonny, still laughing.

"Doesn't count!" exclaimed Billy Bob.

"However," continued Sonny, "I think your paranoia has an element of truth; they're breedin' us for stud, ole buddy. They just don't like to admit it. Doesn't go down well with the Christian ethic."

When Billy Bob got up, he was sullen and inexplicably anxious again. He wiped the sand from his Levi's and football jersey. "I'm tired of wheat germ and yogurt, that's all. Gimme some Twinkies."

Sonny looked soberly at his waterproof Timex, then at the sun, low in the west. The two boys walked back to the bike. After a long silence, Sonny spoke.

"We're supposed to come back with gasoline, you know." He checked Billy Bob's reaction. "And we've missed the church service."

Billy, head down, kicked at the sand as he walked. "Hell, we'll be there for the party. I mean, how often do we get to the beach—once every two years? What'll they do, take away dessert?"

"Doc won't do anything except chew us out," Sonny opined.

They were beside the bike now. Billy Bob put on his cowboy hat, then sat and pulled on a pair of well-used Frye boots. Sonny tied the laces on his sneakers. "So let's get some gas at least." He said this with the thrown-away inflection of a good soft-sell salesman.

Billy's reaction was predictable. "We cleaned out this area two years ago, man!"

"Not along the coast, jerkoff. I thought we'd try northeast of the swamp, Route 1 near Green Swamp . . . where the bomb hit. Must have been something military there. Missile base or something."

That sounded casual enough, thought Sonny. Billy Bob was

44

a big, stubborn fish who had to be maneuvered before landing. If you didn't play him properly and pulled too tight, he'd pop the line.

"That's off-limits—too many rads; make us sterile for sure!" said Billy.

"I brought a Geiger counter. If it's still too hot, we'll cruise right through. We can see how big a hole the bomb made." Sonny paused. "You game, ole stud?"

Sonny almost laughed and blew it when Billy Bob actually peered down anxiously between his own legs. "I don't want it to rot off, that's all!"

"If it does, I'll buy you a new one," Sonny bantered with a "put-on" frown.

Billy Bob had to smile at that; Sonny waited a split second and reeled him in. "There's a porno store in a town we passed through. Good selection. Saw one that looked just right for you."

Billy giggled. Any pleasant reference to his genitalia was worth a yuk. He picked up the big trail bike and put his foot on the starter, nodding, "Yeah?"

"Yeah. Metallic blue with handlebars and a big headlight."

"You fucker!"

Billy guffawed and slammed his boot hard on the kick starter. Sonny shouldered the pack and jumped on the back of the bike. Sand flew as the knobby rear wheel spun, dug in and the machine leaped forward, flying over the dune and into the setting sun.

CHAPTER FIVE

The church doors were open wide. The four-person choir, now in black gowns, stood silhouetted by a deepening saffron sun and chatted in hushed tones. Behind them was Dr. Frank Alden, wearing his ceremonial vestment—a V-shaped soft white ecclesiastical collar over a black robe. And though sometimes he felt misgivings about wearing ceremonial dress, he appreciated the crutch strictly for the sake of his bolstered confidence.

Young Frank Alden had never been "God-fearing" in the Fundamentalist sense. For him there was no white-haired father of Michelangelo design passing out tickets to the hereafter. In fact, throughout medical school at the University of Virginia Frank had avoided formal religion like a rampant social disease. God was not an entity on which to foist off all your problems. Rather, Frank thought, we all have a certain amount of "goodness" in us, and it's got to be each individual's responsibility, not "God's," to be in touch with it. In the name of survival if nothing else. And certainly he was not against mysticism, for the Bible was rich metaphorical poetry for most of his strong beliefs.

When the organ began the processional hymn, the butterflies flapped about his stomach as usual. Here we go again, he thought. Today they'll finally see through me, realize I have nothing to say that I haven't said ten times already. They'll just lift me from my pedestal and carry me out gibbering like an idiot. Oh God, just get me through the dedication, he thought only half jokingly.

The choir sang the hauntingly beautiful (and ancient) Theodoric Petri canticle, "Now the Spring Has Come Again." Frank, being the last person down the aisle, found himself as usual counting the "house." For the first time in four years he came up two souls short.

Anita smiled at him from the organ as the choir filed into the first row of their stalls. Frank stepped toward the pulpit and returned her confidence. Both emotionally and spiritually they were very close.

Kirk and Nancy shared a hymnal. She brushed an overlong bang from her dark, mischievous eyes and whispered to Kirk. "They didn't show up, did they?"

"Who?" said Kirk, his voice more subdued than Nancy's. She could be embarrassing at times.

"You know who," she said almost gleefully. "I hope they bring me something nice this time . . ."

"Something nice?" Kirk repeated mechanically.

"Um-hmm, a strapless suntan, something like that," she said. Dancing eyes belied her flat-bored expression.

Wilkes Bonner, alone in the pew directly behind the teenagers, had had enough. He thrust his big head forward and whispered into Nancy's ear, "Knock it off and sing, damnit!"

But Nancy was unperturbed. She slowly turned her lovely profile to Bonner and blew him a discreet Bronx cheer.

Wilkes restrained an impulse to slug her.

The next twenty minutes went surprisingly smoothly. Frank Alden read Walt Whitman's poem "Son of the Open Road"; there was responsive reading from the prayer books and a short message about Easter Sunday, then Frank walked up into the little pulpit and removed the paper clip from the small cards which composed his sermon. Each Sunday he held this paper clip like a Greek worry bead. In some mysterious way it allowed him to speak his mind. He bowed his head in prayer.

"Ours is the world, the universe and life, if we make it ours by the largeness and strength of our love. Ours is the commonwealth of man, now and tomorrow, building, and yet to be built. Amen."

Frank raised his head and beamed. "Amen, brothers and

sisters! Well, Easter's here again and so are we!" There was a vigorous laugh from the pews. "Good to see you here on this beautiful spring afternoon!"

He paused briefly to make contact with the faces. (Where were Sonny Vandergot and Billy?) He felt another shiver of apprehension, but it passed.

"Five years ago no one was taking serious bets we'd make it this far. Dr. Vandergot's new serum hadn't yet proven itself and the world was suffocating all around us."

He paused again. Something was wrong.

"This was our stand here at the university, we lost friends and relatives to the bomb, to plague and pestilence, to postwar depression. At times we even lost faith in ourselves, in our ability to survive."

Frank looked at the paper clip and felt his palms sweating. Why am I so uncomfortable? he asked himself. But he couldn't pin it on anything. Get on with this, he begged. If you've got something to say, spit it out. They can take it. It was then he realized the extent of his bitterness, the anger he had hidden this morning behind his "nice guy" smile and his ability to rationalize. I'm fucking pissed off, he concluded, and with that his rehearsed words dried up like so many grains of sand blown across a crumbling road. His mind fairly reeked of nuclear graveyards and rotting tortoise maters; his conscience raw and gritty—not for the millions of people dead, but for the damned turtles! For their sterile eggs, their blinded instincts! For the living thing in my wife's womb! My God, he thought, we knew what was happening over twenty-five years ago and we did nothing! Absolutely nothing!

"This Easter Sunday, therefore, is a good time to review our fortunes and misfortunes. Why? Simply because we don't want it to happen again." He took one deep breath and let it out. He felt tears of outrage lick at his eyes. His voice tensed.

"The greatest moral crime of our age was the concealment by science and technology of the true nature of nuclear war. It deprived us as ordinary human beings of the solemn right to sit in judgment of our own fate. It condemned us all unwittingly to the greatest dereliction of conscience the world has ever known. The crust of the earth, animals, microorganisms, seasons, weather and water, the atmosphere and the entire evolutionary process were changed in one giant careless stroke."

49

Yes, he had them now, and they had him. He could see himself mirrored in their faces.

"And because we thought we couldn't adapt, we damn near didn't. Then we found hope, faith in nature, call it what you want, but we came through. And what began as a deathly sick community of forty-three is now a healthy group of fifteen. And we're beginning. Again."

Though Frank's tone had been relatively subdued, his entire body now quivered like a tuning fork. He hadn't meant to be this emotional. As he saw it, his job was to be a moderating influence, someone to lean on. And now his own righteous personal anger had been thrown up at their feet.

Frank wanted to apologize. Instead, he dropped his eyes almost instinctively and did the right thing.

"Now let's have a moment of silent prayer for those not so fortunate as we."

After a full minute, Frank glanced up. Randolph was holding his mother's hand. He sat in his wheelchair on the aisle; she, in a back pew.

"You'll be happy to know I'm done preaching today," said Frank. "I will now pass the buck to Randolph Vandergot, our senator from Georgia."

Every neck strained toward the back of the church.

"Randolph, as you all know, has been my special patient for the past five years. And we've worked very hard together. Last week he asked me if he could give this memorial celebration for his father."

Frank put out his hand palm upward toward Randolph, who nodded, and smiling as broadly as his scarred face permitted, rolled his wheelchair down the aisle. The applause, which was light to begin with, ground to a rocky silence. A slight wobble in the wheelchair was the only sound heard.

"My God, I didn't think that man could even talk . . ." whispered Lynne Jenkins to her husband; both were sitting in the choir stall.

"Shhh . . ." cautioned Roy.

With some difficulty Randolph Vandergot jerked his wheelchair to the front of the church. His mother watched proudly.

Frank stepped down to help Randolph, who was already supporting himself on a metal cane. They walked arm in arm up to the pulpit. Randolph's face, though disfigured, was that of a man reborn. He exuded a youthful, almost childlike aura— but that was somewhat misleading. What you really saw was his slightly disconnected view of life itself, the thread of madness that kept the dark, full-grown fabric at bay.

Frank had worked one-to-one with Randolph Vandergot, first to save the man's body from first-degree flash burns, then to save his mind from walking out on his body. Frank still was unsure why Randolph had survived when so many others in much better condition had died. Perhaps because Randolph had taken the shots a week before anyone else. Also, people with severe flash burns from the bomb developed a certain natural immunity to lethal radiation. This had been true at Hiroshima.

And there was another odd nuclear quirk. People near the burst lost their hair within ten to fifteen days, unless their hair happened to be gray, in which case nothing happened. Burns on those wearing white clothing were much less than on people who wore dark. Randolph had had the good fortune to be wearing a white long-sleeve shirt upon leaving home for church that cool, drizzly Easter Sunday in Washington. And the misfortune to have put on dark trousers, black shoes and socks. One side of his body had been baked from the waist down and the neck up.

Randolph began haltingly, sucking in short breaths from the good side of his mouth. "I'm luckier to be here than most of you. Five years ago my father was alive and seventy-six years old. He was not a famous scientist, but he had a vision. An apocalyptic vision." The tension left his throat now. He could feel his face relax.

"One week before the 'war,' when he was dying and I had come here to be by his side, he insisted that I be inoculated with his serum; for he told me in no uncertain terms that the world as we knew it would soon end." He paused briefly. "I thought Daddy was delirious. I humored him. But before I went back home to Washington to be with my wife and kids, I conceded to his last wishes and received the same treatment as everyone else here. Still I was skeptical. Daddy also wanted to immunize both Congress and the President. The AMA put the quash on that one. The serum was not fully proven, Libya had only threatened to destroy the Suez and nobody took that Libyan idiot seriously." The more Randolph warmed to his subject, the stronger his southern accent became.

"A month or so later I was the only person alive in Washington, D.C., and I remember the last legislator to die just a few days before, Senator Dobson from Maine, he told me, 'Randolph,' he said—we were together in the bomb shelter—

'you're in charge now. Now you're President. I know you always wanted the job.'"

Though Randolph seemed oddly amused by this last remark, the small congregation was horrified.

"And that's how my daddy, Dr. Benjamin Vandergot, caused me, his oldest son, to be chosen the forty-first President of the United States."

Still smiling to himself, Randolph glanced over to Frank, who was now squirming in his seat against the church wall.

"And now we sing our national anthem?"

Frank stood calmly, walked up to the pulpit and took Randolph gently by the arm. "No," he said simply. "Instead, Velma's going to sing 'America, the Beautiful'; that's the song we thought your father would like most."

Randolph grinned at the congregation. "Yes, 'America, the Beautiful' as sung by Miss Velma... Velma Lee Jenkins.

"After that," Randolph added exuberantly, "we've got lots of fun and games planned for the rest of the afternoon, and the party tonight, of course!"

Frank helped Randolph into the first row of pews. They sat down together.

Anita began the introduction on the organ. Velma stood, hymnal in hand, waiting.

Anita gave Velma their prearranged nod.

"Oh, beautiful for spacious skies, for amber waves of grain," began Velma, her voice and tone simple, straightforward.

"For purple mountain majesties above the fruited plain.
America! America! God shed his grace on thee.
And crown thy good with brotherhood
From sea to shining sea."

The words of the song stayed with the congregation for the rest of the day, perhaps because they were fairly humble words for a patriotic song. The lyrics favored brotherhood to "bombs bursting in air," talked about Pilgrim's feet in the wilderness, God mending our flaws, confirming our collective soul with self-control, and even slapped lightly at our excess of riches, "May God their gold refine, till all success be nobleness, And every gain divine."

It was a sensitive, exuberant song, and though you could

quarrel about Indian feet being trampled eventually by Pilgrim boots, it still brought tears to the eye.

Yes, of course it was patriotic, and Frank knew he would get some flak for selecting it, but old Ben Vandergot liked this song. And that was the point today.

CHAPTER SIX

They had taken Route 84 west and turned directly south at Hoboken, Georgia, where Routes 15 and 121 combined. The road was narrower and the sun finally had dipped beyond their view. There would be no more than two hours before darkness.

The gas station was an old-fashioned type with red pumps and glass tops. They cruised around the trees and vines along the gravel shoulder and pulled into the station. Their procedure was a dying ritual. The number of "wet" pumps discovered over the past two years was not more than one in one hundred.

Sonny dropped from the bike and opened his backpack. He withdrew a short crowbar and small pressure foot pump with a length of coiled plastic hose, while Billy Bob searched through the accumulated dirt and vegetation for the access plate to the underground tank.

Billy Bob took the crowbar from Sonny and began to bang it near the base of the pump until he heard a familiar hollow sound. He then dug down until the heavy metal plate was uncovered. The hooked end of the crowbar was applied to the notch in the metal and the plate lifted. When the plate was high enough for a good fingerhold, both Billy and Sonny heaved it aside. Sonny pulled out a long-handled flashlight and shined it into the black cavern.

"Sucker's dry."

Billy Bob nodded, wiped the perspiration from his eyes. "Always another one down the road."

"Down the road," repeated Sonny. They were only fifteen miles from the nuclear bomb site he was so anxious to see.

The Mobil station appeared around the curve before them. Epoxy paint from its once-glistening white walls had been flash-burned down to bare concrete.

The motorcycle pulled up to the one pump that was still standing. Sonny slid off the back seat and yanked an old road map from his Levi's jacket pocket. Billy Bob cut the engine, stood, and looked over Sonny's shoulder at a twist of road that led down the long hill to a roundish swamp lake. Sonny pointed to the lake.

"I bet it was a surface burst. Must have kicked up an awful lot of mud and God knows what else. Trees all around that area are real new."

Billy Bob dropped his eyes. He seemed unnerved. "I'm gonna check for gas. You look for oil. Gimme your pack."

Sonny stripped off his pack and handed it to Billy. Then Sonny ambled over to the station itself, which was mostly rubble. A kick at some loose concrete uncovered a spark plug and a blistered can of Simoniz Wax. Billy Bob lifted the tank cover out front.

Sonny went to the toilet and basin, which no longer were separated from the rest of the building. Something scuttled through the underbrush outside. He stepped through the partially broken wall to check it out. A jackrabbit froze momentarily, then hopped into a thicket.

Sonny smiled and turned to go back through the wall. Suddenly *he* froze. Baked into the cement on the half wall was the image of a person walking—just a gray shadow smudge on the cement, the barest outline.

Billy Bob, meanwhile, took out the flashlight and shined it into the buried gas tank. A small amount of gasoline was reflected in the beam. Billy grinned broadly and lifted his head to yell for Sonny, when he himself was called. The urgency of the shout sent him running to the side of the station.

"What . . . ?"

Sonny gestured to the grim atomic epitaph on the wall.

"Sucker must have been going to the bathroom," he said slyly.

Billy Bob did not move for a few seconds; then he turned his head away and shuddered. His mother and father had been vacationing near Cape Canaveral when the first missiles fell on strategic targets.

Billy Bob walked stiffly back toward the bike. Sonny followed, wanting to say something to make his friend less upset, yet not knowing what to say.

Far below them, hovering in the dark shadows of a large oak tree and camouflaged by damp moss and fungus, a half man on two stout legs shuffled forward to observe the boys siphoning gasoline into cans on either side of the bike's rear fender.

Sonny glanced at his watch while holding the tube into the gasoline tank and pumping with his foot. Gasoline bubbled to the top of the can. Sonny stopped pumping, squeezed the hose and stuck it into the other tank. Billy was squatting Indian style looking out over the meadow across the highway and down the hill. He tossed some pebbles in front of him.

Sonny spoke offhandedly. "Must have been a military installation of some type down there." Billy Bob continued flipping stones into the asphalt road.

Sonny's voice was flat monotone. "My guess is there were missile silos in that meadow. Should be some souvenirs down there."

"I've seen enough souvenirs. That thing full yet?" Billy Bob stood and frowned at the bike.

"Almost," said Sonny. "Look, Billy, relax . . . what we saw back on that wall was just a ghost, not even . . . we've got less than an hour before dark if you want to look around."

Billy Bob's face turned white with rage. "You're crazy, you know that? For a bright guy, you got a damn screw loose. That was a person back there! Christ, my father owned a goddamned gas station!"

Gasoline boiled to the top of the second tank. Sonny pinched the plastic hose again and pulled the long end from the black hole in the ground, letting it drain while he retrieved it.

"I'm sorry, Billy," he said after a long, painful pause.

Billy Bob said nothing. He stared blankly at the darkening sky, thinking about his folks. A few choked words finally struggled forth. "Sometimes it gets very lonely, you know . . ."

Sonny put on his pack. "I know."

Billy Bob pitched one last rock far down the hill. Then he straddled the trailbike and kicked the starter.

"Just get on," he muttered wearily.

In the fading light of the hillside, the man-thing could see two creatures, one behind the other, traveling quickly down the hillside on top of something red that made a low, unpleasant, rumbling noise. He retreated farther into the darkness of shadows, merging his body totally with the lush vegetation.

The Yamaha hopped through the foot-high grass, skirting the young palmettos and dwarf oak trees, contorted as if from some unseen storm. Bright green resurrection ferns, sucking up the leaf mold and dust from the deep-grooved bark of the oaks, wriggled up twisted limbs. All plant life here was an uncanny green in the fading light of day. Fractured logs lay damp and humid, covered with green earlike lichens.

The riders ducked low limbs of red bay and sweet gum trees, and the bike burst into a new clearing.

A tall shadow fell across their path. The bike slid to a halt.

Sticking thirty feet up from the ground and silhouetted against the western sky was a broken cylindrical object garishly covered in mottled green.

"Oh, God!" cried Sonny.

They both stared mesmerized at the shattered ICBM as if it were a spaceship from another world. The tip, or payload, of the missile lay below—a tangle of wires, broken canisters and ripped metal stewing in a soft bed of bubbling muck. The shank of the missile was split wide open. Fungus had crawled into every crack and hole of the metal skin.

Awestruck still, the two boys stood motionless astride the bike, hearts palpitating. The bike engine had stopped. The high-pitched human scream of a nearby southern oak frog softened to a nervous whimper.

The entire area that had once been ten missile silos was at once surreal, dreamlike, an ancient burial ground. Cement contours of blastproof entrances had long since been molded and reshaped by thickets, shrubs, hollies, huckleberries, fetterbushes and vines interweaving. Bright red lichens. Black bamboo vines with formidable spines. Farther west, at the base of Trail Ridge, tall, gaunt cypresses with muscular roots gripped the horizon like watchful crows. Beyond would be the southern end of Cowhouse Island called Gum Slough.

They were too low now to see the bomb's impact area. A

bull alligator groaned somewhere nearby. Billy Bob's jaw tensed—his first outward reaction.

"I think we'd better go."

Sonny was still entranced, unhearing.

"Our nuke here must have been blasted just as it was preparing to launch. I wonder why it didn't explode?"

Billy Bob winced. "Don't know and don't intend to find out. This ain't no goddamn physics class. Come on!"

Sonny walked over to where the business end of the missile was splayed open in the muck. Trying not to get his sneakers too wet, he picked up a stick and poked at one of the ruptured canisters.

Billy Bob was scared, impatient. "Christ, get outta there, Sonny. That must be loaded with radiation!"

Sonny hooked the V end of the stick into the canister and pulled it toward him. Billy Bob leaned in closer.

"What's all that bubbling?"

The canister was nearly close enough for them to read the military inscription on its side.

"Probably methane from decaying vegetation—marsh gas."

Sonny had the canister on dry ground. He scraped away the slime with his stick to reveal a military description of the ingredients: "Enteropathica Hominus III." The company trademark was listed below: "ARMY LABORATORY FOR BACTERIOLOGICAL WARFARE, Frederick, Maryland."

Sonny stared long and hard at the broken canister, then glanced down at his feet. Some of the muck had already soaked into his basketball shoes. Looking very pale, he turned to Billy.

"This is why it didn't explode—it wasn't a bomb. It was bacteria for export to Russia. But instead they must have blown it up right in our faces."

Sonny dropped the stick and tiptoed out of the wet area toward the bike.

"I'm going to use the emergency CB to call in."

Billy Bob flushed. "Do that and we're in real trouble. You know we're not supposed to be in this area."

"Look, damnit, didn't you hear what I said? I don't know what five years of sitting here has done to that stuff in the canisters. But I'm sure as hell not going to take a chance! The whole community could be contaminated!"

"What?" Billy Bob's temples pounded with a sudden violent headache. Sonny removed the CB microphone from the motorcycle.

At the receiver end of the transmission a special tape deck recorded everything that Sonny was saying; then it clicked off like a teletype. The church office was empty.

Sonny returned the mike to its compartment and fastened it with a short elastic cord. Billy Bob was about to start the engine when a hand touched his shoulder.

"I thought I saw something big move in those trees out there."

A breeze blew, catching the long blond hair under Billy Bob's cowboy hat. His nose wrinkled in distaste.

"God Almighty, did you smell that? Something's dead!"

"Yeah, and..." Sonny looked carefully into the red bay and gum trees.

"And what...?" Billy Bob asked.

"All the swamp noises have stopped."

Both boys stood quietly, listening and staring into the nearby hammock. Branches rustled gently where no wind blew.

"Let's get our butts out of here, Billy."

"Right on, babe. We're gone."

Billy Bob's boot heel hit the kick starter. He accelerated viciously and the motor roared like a giant watchdog. Dirt flew back at the trees as the machine ground up toward Trail Ridge and Route 1.

CHAPTER SEVEN

Velma Lee was wearing a white camisole of her own design and her best tight jeans. She had just set thirteen places on the checkered oilcloth table by the gazebo and debated whether to lay out two extra ones for Sonny and Billy Bob.

Somehow, the swimming and running and jumping contests of the afternoon had not been as much fun without the two boys. It was certainly no fun watching Kirk walk away with all the annual events. He was almost a professional. Sometimes Sonny could beat him in running. Billy could take him Indian wrestling. But nobody could outdazzle him generally. Velma Lee found herself especially angry with Sonny. In some way inexplicable to herself, she felt that he had let her down.

Through her thick glasses she could see Dr. Alden and Nathan placing Coleman lanterns on low-hanging limbs of the surrounding live oaks. The ground here was cushy underfoot. The trunks of the two trees sheltering the gazebo were each at least twelve feet wide, evergreens and full of sweet acorns. She had experimented with eating the acorns like chestnuts, even pressing out the oil the way the Indians used to do. The oil was great for cooking in hominy.

The small egg-shaped leaves on the tree grew from the

gnarled dips of limb. They were smooth, tough and shiny, and in spring the branches dropped old leaves for new ones. Two landed just now with dry clicks on the oilcloth in front of her.

Mother Nature's grand designs were beautifully obvious in Velma's knitting and crocheting. She was considered the artist of the community; she had that kind of eye for things. She could see how everything connected, how dissimilar colors fit together in harmony. Her large, luminous, green eyes were like her father's, except hers had sustained the wonder of youth, particularly for God's green world and its creatures.

She had designed the little Japanese gazebo, built just last year overlooking the spring pond. Overflow from the pond escaped through a small algae stream down a coarse sandbank and into a swamp stream the color of Dr. Pepper. The tall cypresses, whose thick roots anchored the trembling mass of peat, sand and water on the opposite side of the stream, looked so wonderfully mysterious this time of evening.

Velma set the two extra places. She knew the two boys would be back tonight, if for no other reason than to eat her mother's delicious peach pies.

Velma's mother was just now placing the pies on a serving table to cool. Everybody was busy. Her father put up colorful paper streamers around the pavilion and curled them over the oak limbs. Now and then he would nip at his wine bottle. He was drinking more lately. His battered Oklahoma fiddle lay on the smooth wooden gazebo floor. Soon he'd pick it up and play some square-dance tunes. Call them too, in his high nasal voice.

Normally, meals were prepared in the church kitchen, and everybody ate around the large oak table in the next room.

Looking up the hill, Velma saw Nancy and Kirk walk down from the church carrying the big stainless-steel pot full of home-made high-protein spaghetti. She liked Kirk but didn't fancy Nancy. Fancy Nancy thinks she's hot tomatoes, thought Velma. Kirk is okay—dumb, but cute. Sonny was the one everyone had their eyes on. Everyone. Maybe even her mother. Sonny was very handsome, possibly too much so; and, of course, intelligent like all the other Vandergots, except Senator Randolph. Brother! The nightmares she'd had from looking at that face. Hard to believe he was Sonny's father.

Sonny! What a hunk! He had pinched her cheek once when they were all swimming in the pond last summer. "Can't wait for you to grow up," he said. "You're gonna be prettier than

62

your mama, Velma Lee!" Then I spit water at him through my chipped front tooth and he ducked me till I darn near drowned, she thought wisftully.

How could he have said that? I wasn't pretty then, and I'm not now. Just tall with no boobs, no butt and no hips, and my glasses magnify the clump of freckles around my nose and eyes. In fact, I think I'm rather ugly. How could he say that?

Velma's mother called for her to come to the serving table.

Velma nodded. I'm coming, Mother, she said to herself. Now that I'm fourteen, must sex raise its hideous head? I suppose that's what Sonny wants. That's what Mother says all men want.

Except Eric. Though I really wouldn't call Eric a man. Not even a boy. He's more of an android. Sexless Eric. My God, Mother, if you think I'm such a serious person, you should see Eric when we study together in the Chandler library at night. He's going to be an immunologist like Dr. Alden. Maybe I'll be a biologist. Eric *never* takes his nose out of his damn books!

"What, Mother?"

Lynne Jenkins, dressed in a bright red halter and gypsy skirt, was doing a nervous fan dance around four lovely pies. She was trying desperately to keep the flies at bay.

"Honey, take this and keep those filthy things away while I find a cover, okay?" She handed Velma the fan.

"Okay, Mama." Reluctantly Velma took the fan and began to wave it around. She was about to enjoy another favorite daydream when a small white hand reached up from under the work table and tried to grab a pie.

Velma raised her weapon and swatted the hand hard. The fingers curled instantly, then disappeared with an accompanying yelp. Velma Lee lifted the cotton tablecloth and hissed, "That's enough, Henry Baldwin! Next time I'll break your greasy fingers! Now get out from under there!"

The moon was higher now against a charcoal sky. The motorcycle, headlight lit, bounced along a hardtop, then stopped and paused at an intersection. Sonny yelled to Billy Bob over the engine:

"Go right on 121! It's a shortcut!"

"You sure?"

"That's what the map says."

"What if a nuke has shortened that shortcut?"

"Well, that's why we're riding a dirt bike, right? Let's do it!"

The narrow road ran directly through the eastern side of the Okefenokee past old Camp Cornelia. Since there had been none of the usual winter fires set by careless campers in the past five years, the swamp had made incredible growth both upward and outward.

They passed an abandoned car with a large pine tree pushing up through its broken windshield. At intervals the trees and vines on either side of the road connected to make a great dark tunnel that shut out the starred sky completely.

Billy Bob thought the world was closing over, that they were being buried in moist green darkness. Furious that they hadn't returned the way they had come, Billy fought to keep his mouth shut. But his eyes were wide open. To the gaping holes in the old tar road. To sharp-toothed brambles that clawed at his jacket and trousers. To night flowers so sweet that he almost gagged on their sticky perfume.

The eyes of swamp animals flowed luminous in the headlights. A ten-foot cottonmouth slithered across the warm black surface.

The lively breeze of the afternoon had been snuffed out by the giant breath of night. For ten minutes not a word was exchanged between them. Then Sonny leaned forward close to Billy Bob's ear.

"I figure we'll sleep in a house near the university tonight, call Doc in the morning and ask him what . . . ."

Suddenly the front wheel of the bike smacked into a deep crater.

"Jesus . . . careful!"

"Don't tell me how to drive the goddamn bike!"

Up ahead in the thin glare of the single headlight something two-legged scuttled across the road. Billy Bob caught the movement from the corner of his eye and strained to see through the gloom.

"I think I saw . . . !"

He didn't finish. The front tire plowed into another trough and the bike weaved drunkenly.

"Shit!!!" exclaimed Billy.

"Yeah, shit!" agreed Sonny.

Billy Bob brought the Yamaha to a wobbly stop, kicked the stand into an upright position, then knelt to examine the front tire, pushing at its softness with indignant fingers.

"Be flat in a minute. Hope you brought patches."

"No . . . I thought you . . ."

Billy Bob smiled grimly. "I got some . . . for all your brains, ole buddy . . ."

The guttural moan from somewhere up ahead cut him short. Both boys felt the shiver of adrenaline shoot up their spines. Billy Bob recovered first. "Another bull alligator, huh?"

"Could have been a bear."

"Nuh-uh."

Sonny yanked a screwdriver and a wrench from his pack and handed them to Billy Bob. Sonny also took out a flashlight. As Billy cut the engine, Sonny flicked the beam into the swamp on either side of them.

Billy Bob pried at the wheel rim with the screwdriver.

Sonny was talking. "That trapper Oral Jarvis used to say bears in the swamp sometimes bite off chunks of pine, let the tree bleed for a day or two and roll in it. Then they roll in sand and leaves. He said they look pretty weird afterwards."

Billy Bob had half the tire off. "Didn't walk like a bear. Didn't talk like one, either."

"What happened to the zoos?"

"What do you mean?"

Sonny shined the light up the road again. "Gorillas, for instance."

"Year, sure," said Billy Bob. "Hey, do me a favor and shine me some of that. I can't see what the fuck I'm doin' here."

The thing from the swamp moved slowly along the shoulder of the asphalt, taking cover in the soft foliage that had usurped the road. Stalking between moonlight and shadow, it was hard to discern. However, it was coming closer to the flashlight and to the two strangers crouched around the strange red machine.

Billy Bob had the tire off the rim and was scanning the inner tube. Sonny still held the flashlight. Billy poked a certain spot with his finger.

"There . . ."

Billy Bob dug into his jacket pocket and pulled out a roll of patches. "Damn lucky it didn't blow."

The man-thing loped forward at a more rhythmic pace, never quickly but sure of its strength, confident on its own turf. Then it stopped. Silently brushing aside the leaves of small branches, it glanced through cold, fishlike eyes at the two humans.

Billy lay the yellow patch across the dark slash in the rubber and pressed down hard.

"Hope that holds. Would ya hand me the pump?"

Sonny reached under the bike and retrieved the small hand pump. He handed it to Billy Bob. Billy fastened the hose to the air valve and began pumping rapidly.

Finally he stopped, thumped the tire once and unscrewed the valve connection. As he stood, the thundering frog chorus that had accompanied them through most of the swamp slowed gradually, then stopped as if someone had turned the volume to "off." The leopard frogs, tree frogs, rain frogs, peepers— all the forty-odd varieties that populate the Okefenokee—now were silent.

Sonny and Billy Bob both tensed. The silence was deafening.

"Let's get a move on," said Billy Bob anxiously.

Then another distant moaning sound was heard. This time it was more like a chorus.

"Bears, alligators, my ass," said Billy. He bent over to make the last few turns of the wheel nut with his wrench, then straightened, and holding the wrench like a weapon, looked hard at Sonny.

"You drive. I'll ride shotgun."

Sonny nodded, tossed his leg over the bike. Billy Bob stuffed the wrench into his belt and climbed on behind.

As the motorcycle roared down the dark swamp road, the voyeur emerged carefully from the woods' edge.

Now astride the road, legs spread, it threw its arms wide and roared.

The motorcycle engine drowned out all noise from the swamp. Sonny pulled a pair of yellow "pilot" glasses from his Levi's jacket pocket and pressed them onto his nose. With his sleeve he wiped a sticky mess of tiny corpses from his perspiring forehead. The rubber on the handlebar grips felt hot and damp against his palms, and he strained to see through or around the obstacles ahead.

The road took a sharp turn. The headlight illuminated a section completely covered with bushes and small stunted trees, where pavement was almost nonexistent. Sonny eased on both hand and foot brake. He shifted down. His eyes searched for an easy trail through the vegetation.

Suddenly from the undergrowth directly to his front, a figure jumped out of hiding and lurched toward the oncoming motorcycle, its arms waving wildly in front of its face.

"Jesus!" shrieked Sonny, his blood turning to ice.

Billy was startled too. He raised his wrench as the figure stumbled toward them, trying to avoid the bright headlight that burned at its eyes.

"Give him the light, blind him!" screamed Billy Bob.

"Jesus!" Sonny had frozen as solid as a startled rabbit, his mouth dry as a sand pit.

"Shift down!" ordered Billy Bob. The figure was almost on top of them.

Sonny only quivered, his eyes glazed over, his mouth slack.

"Turn it left!" wailed Billy. "For Christ's sake, Sonny!"

At the last possible second, Sonny marshalled his senses. He jerked the handlebars left, avoiding a head-on collision.

As the huge encrusted hand reached for them, Billy cracked the wrench across its shoulder. The thing fell, wailing in anger like a wounded alligator.

"Jesus!" Sonny repeated, panic-stricken, and now looking for an exit. Billy Bob's voice roared into his ears.

"Wake up, Sonny, goddamnit, there's more ahead!"

Sonny brought the motorcycle to a stop. In a loose phalanx across the road appeared twelve nightmarish shapes of semi-men. The fungus that completely covered their bodies glistened in the moonlight. They look almost like trees, Sonny thought. He yanked off his bug-stained glasses and tossed them away. When he glanced back again, the trees were motionless!

"Now what?" Sonny demanded in a high, tense voice.

"Blow the horn," answered Billy, "blink your lights, open full throttle! Make us a hole!"

Sonny pushed hard on the horn and blinked the lights up and down. There was absolutely no movement. "They're not moving," he whispered through his teeth.

"Go right through those bushes on the left side," said Billy Bob quickly. "I think I see an embankment."

Billy Bob heard something behind them. The one he'd smacked was loping toward them.

Sonny tensed up again. "I'm not used to this bike, Billy!"

Billy snarled, "Shift down and hit it, man! We can't switch now!"

The motorcycle was less than twenty yards from the leading grotesque. They were losing precious seconds.

"Okay, move it or get off, damnit!" Billy Bob threatened. He could smell the familiar stink behind him.

"Okay, okay!" Sonny gibbered. His right hand jerked counterclockwise on the throttle. The machine leaped forward and

67

cut sharply to the left. It thundered off the shoulder of the broken road and ground its way through reeds and willows up a five-foot embankment.

The gnarled figures came to life, wheeling in tandem to block this end run, two of them already clawing their way up the short hill.

Sonny looked down in horror. He was coming apart again. Then he popped the clutch, and the bike jumped forward and stalled. Billy Bob was thrown to the ground. A Jeep can slid off the rear fender and onto the road.

Billy Bob recovered at once. He snatched up his wrench. He leaped to his feet, and crazy-brave with fear, screamed his challenge to the approaching monsters.

"Come and get it, suckers, whatever the hell you are!"

As one of the thick spore-covered paws reached for his boot, Billy Bob smashed the paw with the wrench. The thing screamed, and in spasm drew back its mauled extremity.

"Get the bike started!" cried Billy. A second figure was climbing the hill.

Sonny kicked the starter so hard he nearly broke his leg. Nothing. The bike was stalled.

The mob closed in, moving slowly but with strength, and willfully, an awkward precision to their movement, never mindless but like a slightly demented football team in slow motion.

Billy swung his wrench wide. The blow glanced off the head of the second foul-smelling monstrosity. The thing lost its balance and toppled.

Sonny's foot ached. Half his sneaker was torn off from kicking furiously at the starter. The circle of trees was tightening around them. A third freak stalked up the incline. Sonny shoved his bruised foot frantically against the metal.

"Start, damnit!!! Start, you son-of-a-bitch!!!"

The engine sputtered slowly at first, then exploded to life. The headlight flashed.

"Shine the light in his eyes!" howled Billy Bob.

Sonny twisted the handlebars around for a first good look at the monster. It was a horrible but short-lived portrait. It was horrible because it was like looking at nothing but a dead and rotting part of a tree thickly covered with fungus and lichen. Then the thing shielded its eyes with a limblike arm.

Billy Bob swung the wrench at the arm, beating it and its

owner to the ground. A menacing roar went up from the group in the rear. Reserves committed, the horde charged en masse.

Sonny had the motorcycle up. Billy handed him the slippery, bloody wrench and leaped onto the seat. Sonny climbed onto the back and tried to hold on. The motorcycle did a wheelie. It caromed down the hill into the thick of the charging army.

The two opposing forces converged, challenging one another as if in some ancient form of personal combat. In seeming slow motion the bike, now gathering speed, smacked into this mass of not-too-solid flesh. As in professional football, a hole opened for a moment, then closed quickly.

Many huge arms and thick bodies yanked the riders from their seats.

The empty motorcycle zoomed riderless across the road, off the shoulder and crashed into the swamp.

Screams from the road were muffled and bloodcurdling. Only the occasional human arm or leg protruded from the writhing piles of fungoid skin.

The last thing Sonny remembered was staring up at the nearly full moon, then nothing but wetness and the sickening, suffocating odor of alien beings piled on top of his limp body.

When his eyes finally closed, he saw a prairie of swamp grass waving back and forth rhythmically as the beat of a heart or the force of the sea.

CHAPTER EIGHT

Eric closed the tap of the large cider barrel atop a stainless-steel counter in the church kitchen. Stuffing corks into two earthenware jugs, he raised them to his shoulders by small, thick handles and made for a kitchen door that opened onto the mall.

When he put down his load to grasp the doorknob, he could hear a faint pinging sound—the warning bleeper in Frank's administrative office.

Down a dark hall he moved.

Inside the office an alert red eye from the emergency message console illuminated a huge oak desk with blood-tinted books, papers and paraphernalia.

A rising moon lit Eric as he walked down the meadow hill toward the pavilion with its safe, bright lights and laughter.

Much farther up the hill, not far from the cemetery behind the gymnasium, Scarlett watched the lone, distant figure hobble through meadow grass under a heavy load.

The noise and glow from the little pavilion was at once distracting and comforting. The laughter made it difficult to pinpoint a large alligator she knew to be lurking somewhere in a nearby gulley, but the proximity of people could be helpful in case of emergency.

Scarlett did not actually "think" this; it was intuited. "Old Sharptooth" had been a bother for the past three nights, but till now, she had somehow managed to checkmate his ever-stalking reptilian moves.

She sniffed the cool air for his familiar scent of musk, then darted forward to nip at woolly flanks, to gather her sheep into a tighter protective knot, to herd them closer to the laughing people cloistered below.

Henry Baldwin sat twiddling his fork, smearing the soggy remains of his peach pie back and forth across his flowered dinner plate. He'd had four helpings.

Blah, blah, blah, he thought as Roy Jenkins, his stepfather, began telling a second after-dinner joke to the captive audience at the long picnic table.

Henry was two places to the right of his stepfather, with Velma in between.

She looks pretty tonight, Henry thought.

Tonight he even liked the chipped front tooth that gave her mouth a quirky, lopsided smile. He wanted to reach out and touch her soft skin, maybe even kiss her on a dimpled cheek, but instead his hand went to his lap beneath the table, to the ball of damp spaghetti rolled up in a paper napkin.

Maybe now, he thought. Maybe now, while Velma was looking the other way, kind of dreamy-eyed.

Henry slid his chair back slowly and stared down at Velma's favorite running shoes, which she had removed during the course of the ceremonial dinner. Her bare feet now gripped the wooden rung of her folding chair.

Henry nervously awaited the next burst of laughter. When it came, he dropped his fork beneath the table, then dove down to retrieve it, pouring his cold bag of spaghetti into Velma's shoes. This accomplished, he surfaced quickly, his sticky pie fork in a hand covered with a layer of black humus. Velma turned and glanced at the fork. Henry, seeing her surprised expression, popped it into his mouth and made a big show of smacking his lips.

"Disgusting," she muttered.

Henry smiled with satisfaction. Velma turned back to her father, who was being accorded another laugh.

"But seriously," continued Roy Jenkins, "*he* is the man

most responsible for licking our yellow fever and Rocky Mountain spotted fever, not to mention so many other diseases we've had to deal with."

Blah, blah, blah, thought Henry. He hated to sit still. He hated to listen to anybody, particularly his stepfather.

"A couple of us had our ruptured appendix removed by his steady hand," said Jenkins. "He's worked patiently with a few mentally depressive flipouts, myself included."

Henry glanced over to Randolph, asleep in his wheelchair. Probably drunk, he thought. Likes hard cider.

"He taught us how to refertilize our soil, to grow almost normal prewar fruit and vegetables, raise horses and sheep that now produce healthy offspring, and . . . and throughout the past five years, helped us maintain a semblance of law, order and goodwill."

Roy Jenkins grinned with brimming camaraderie.

"And, although we agreed from the beginning not to hand out such awards, tonight we're gonna ease around that rule. Doc, will you come pick up your present?"

Just across the table Henry saw Anita Alden lean over to kiss her husband. He saw Dr. Alden turn red. Doc actually blushed. Then, as everyone applauded, Doc, with a mournful expression, stood up shaking his head. And though he tried to sit right back down again, they forced him with their applause around the table to receive their gift.

Henry still was bored. No more words, please. Just open it. Maybe I'll get drunk too, he thought. He tipped the white clay jug in front of him, the one Eric had brought down the hill a few minutes ago, and poured himself a glass of cloudy-brown apple cider.

When he saw Eric, who was now sitting next to Mrs. Alden, watching him, he made a small, ludicrous face. But Eric, who was still out of breath, studiously avoided his gaze. Anita then leaned toward Eric as if she had forgotten to ask him something.

"Any word from our two delinquents?"

Eric barely nodded, his face rigid.

"Something wrong?"

"I better talk to Doc," Eric said darkly.

Anita frowned but asked no more questions. Henry thought nothing of this. He watched as his stepfather handed Doc Alden the large gift-wrapped box. Doc Alden did a quick foot shuffle and set the box on the table.

"Get me out of the pulpit or away from a chalkboard," he

said quietly, "and I'm never sure what to say." He paused briefly and choked up while still looking at the gift. "I thought we'd all agreed on . . . no, damnit, this isn't fair."

"Maybe you should just go ahead and open it, Doc," said Jenkins.

"Very good idea," said Frank finally. "Moments like this I definitely need something to do with my hands."

Opening the envelope on top of the package first, he took out the handwritten card and read aloud: " 'Just a few things we know you can use.' Well . . ."

Well? thought Henry. Go ahead, rip it open.

Frank's fingers worked at the paper and colored ribbon. The top came free of tissue paper. He lifted it from the box.

Henry waited anxiously. Frank looked down for a long moment. When he glanced up, his eyes were glazed and moist.

"Thank you . . . thank you so much . . ." he said simply.

Inside the box was a handmade object crafted by each person in the community: a tiny sweater of lambs' wool, a hat to match, the rattle (Henry had given) fashioned from a small dried orange and yellow gourd, a patchwork blanket, miniature leather moccasins, a cardboard animal mobile, a stuffed red flannel kitten with button eyes—fourteen articles in all; everything for a newborn.

Henry actually laughed aloud when Roy Jenkins shouldered his fiddle; as much as he disliked the man, he loved his music.

With arms and fingers flying, Roy sang "For He's a Jolly Good Fellow" with the zeal of a strong country caller.

This was a moment of tribute and hope. Of pride; for everyone but Henry. He backed away from the table when people rose to sing.

Beneath the table, poised on the wooden rungs of her chair, Velma's naked feet slipped into the shoes beneath her and sank smoothly into damp spaghetti. Up like mud between her toes squished the soft pasta.

And as thunderbolts of shock and outrage flashed through her sentimental tears of moments before, she spun quickly to her right, her fists knotted. But sweet Henry was long gone.

Anita flinched when the cold metal head of the stethoscope touched her throbbing stomach. She lay naked on her back in their small bedroom apartment just off the mall. Frank was severely disturbed, she could see that. And although she wanted to calm him down, when he was distant like this, she wasn't sure how to do that.

Very still, Frank sat on the bed next to Anita and listened to the rapid heartbeat of their child. Finally he removed the stethoscope.

"That's about right," he said, then was silent again and staring out at the night through the high window of the old-fashioned room. Cold and unsympathetic, the universe winked back its ordered, predictable light.

"I should never have let those boys go today." His head still was turned away.

Anita reached for his hand. She wanted to say something wise, something to alleviate that familiar depression now leeching its way back into their lives.

"They were just curious about the war, Frank," was all she could think to say. Then, as an afterthought, "Please go to sleep now. You need rest . . . for tomorrow."

"Yeah," muttered Frank. A moment later he stood up from the bed and put the stethoscope into the small drawer of the night table. On top of the table a single hurricane candle flickered hypnotically.

Anita watched as Frank slowly squeezed the wick between his thumb and forefinger. The flame blackened his skin.

"Lord, I hope it's not another plague," he whispered, and when she saw that he could not look her in the face, she lowered her eyes and felt his isolation overwhelm her.

At seven o'clock the following morning, Frank, Nathan and Roy Jenkins left the back door of the university hospital clad in rubberized U.S. Army chemical/bacteriological warfare suits. The day was hot, sultry.

Definite possibility of rain, thought Frank. He opened the driver door and placed on the floorboards the mask and gloves he was carrying.

"Back to square one," he said half aloud, removing a road map from his rubber pocket. It was boiling inside the suit, but he couldn't complain. He knew that Roy and Nathan felt as uncomfortable as he.

Which way would the kids have come home from Green Swamp? The freeway would be safest, the least obstructed. He had no idea what shape the smaller roads were in. He, himself, hadn't been in that area for almost two years. And no one, to his knowledge, had traveled as far northeast as the old missile site. That was out-of-bounds, always had been. You certainly didn't go monkeying around in radioactive areas you knew nothing about. That's *why* it was out-of-bounds!

Germ warfare! He scowled. God, we even had to compete with the Russians on that sorry level.

"I put extra oxygen bags in back," said Nathan. "We've got plenty of air."

"Good," replied Frank. He was sweating like a Turk as he turned the ignition key and the four-cylinder engine hiccuped to life.

On the road, no one spoke except to discuss directions. Hard going for a truck, even this little Toyota. And they certainly couldn't afford a bad accident. Not now.

So they took it easy. Frank drove slowly, moving around the largest potholes, skirting the small slash pines poking up through the asphalt, monitoring the water gauge because the radiator had a tendency to overheat.

Now, on the freeway, two hours later, they had found no trace of the two boys. Frank floored the accelerator, looked at the wide road ahead. Driving without obstacles made him feel almost giddy; probably the only good feeling he'd had since last night. But the depression still was there—something indescribably morbid gnawing away at five years of hard-earned confidence. Nameless anxiety was the worst. The absolute worst.

Everyone agreed that the boys wouldn't have tried to come directly home. They would have holed up somewhere first, then radioed in.

Interstate 95 still stretched out straight before them like a giant runway.

My Lord, thought Frank, in a few thousand years when all the vehicles revert to dust, will anyone begin to understand what these monstrous cement trails once were used for?

They left 95, taking 84 west; then drove south on Route 121.

A light rain beaded the windshield, and Frank eased up on the accelerator. Colorful lichen, perfectly adapted to the new terrain, gripped the relatively bare spots of cement road like slippery limpets.

A battered Exxon station stood on their right when they stopped. They climbed out and looked down across the meadow. At first no obvious missile silos were visible.

They honked their horn and yelled for Sonny and Billy. No answer. Only echoes.

Then the rain approached as a solid gray wall, hissing at the ground like an army of angry serpents.

Donning their birdlike pleximasks and their gloves and wearing oxygen packs on their hips, they scoured the meadow below.

At length they discovered motorcycle tracks, the ruptured Minuteman, the canisters, the silo complex—yes, everything that checked out with the recorded message.

But no boys.

Tired and discouraged, they sealed fungus and bacteria samples in specimen bags and took photographs. Behind a spread of red gum trees, Jenkins focused on a strange footprint which he at the time assumed to be that of an alligator.

They left two hours before sundown.

Nathan saw it first—just a red splotch through the high saw grass along the side of the road.

Most of the way along Route 121 they had had to break out the machetes and whack away at fetter bushes, sedges, shrubs and even small trees.

Now cypresses, over 400 years old, towered 120 feet over their heads. Plant life in this new area was multi storied, creeping in all directions.

"One of their gas cans," said Nathan. They stood around the red object silently, machetes in hand, and watched the gasoline drip from its bent top.

"SONNY! BILLY!" cried Roy Jenkins. Again, no answer. Only a distorted chorus of swamp frogs and toads preparing for the oncoming night: chirrups, grunts, bleats, squeaks and even something that emitted a metallic clang.

Frank's voice was flat through the filter box in his peaked mask. "Five after six," he said, looking at the watch strapped to his wrist and tugging at the rubber sleeve chafing his armpit. They would not be able to remove their airtight clothing before scrubbing down with disinfectant at the hospital.

"Hard to imagine leaving something as precious as gasoline behind," said Nathan.

The fact that they had, gave Frank chills. Something *had* happened here. And despite the dimming light, they could make out a few signs of a struggle: branches broken, grass smashed flat.

Jenkins retrieved his Nikon from the Toyota and began taking flash shots.

"Over here!" yelled Nathan from inside the treeline.

Frank and Roy reared up like two frightened olive-drab birds.

"Where?" yelled Frank.

"Here!" said Nathan. "I can see the bike!"

Nathan was standing on an embankment among the deeply shadowed cypresses; he motioned Frank and Roy toward him.

Nathan pointed with his flashlight to a dim green mass of floating algae. Handlebars gleamed in the light.

"Goddamn, Frank, you think they're in there?" asked Jenkins anxiously.

Frank said nothing. He began to explore the levels of swamp with his own flashlight. And what he saw disturbed him: The tall cypresses rose into the air, blocking light to the water; their enormous roots twisted and turned as if damned by their maker to endure eternal suffering.

We're inside a great natural cathedral, he thought. A dark, living cathedral on a primordial sea.

Something slapped the water beneath a giant cypress about twenty feet to their front. Both flashlights caught the frantic ripples and tried to explore the gaps between the thick roots, some as thick as a man's leg.

What they could not see was Sonny's head. It had been propped up like a moldering stump among the roots when he'd heard them calling. Perhaps "calling" was not the right word. The vaguely familiar voices were paging him from another dimension. But he *had* managed to open his eyes, to gape open his mouth without choking on the slime beneath his chin. And he *had* tried to answer them with whatever empathetic part of his brain still functioned.

But the amorphous thing behind him simply slapped down his head, thrusting it deeper into the gelatinous soup, until the boy's mind again was semiconscious and subservient.

Billy had adapted immediately. Sonny, the more intelligent, had gone the hard way.

An alligator groaned nearby.

Seconds later, as the rich cacophony of swamp animal sounds slowly diminished, an awesome silence prevailed. The men looked from one to another. Somehow this was *not* a natural phenomenon; it was profoundly disturbing.

"We're going," said Doc. And he said this loudly, not only to his own men but also to the presence he felt out there.

"We'll come back tomorrow, when it's daylight."

Slowly they backed away. The rain had stopped. A rosy glimmer of setting sun reflected through a break in the low western clouds. They were thankful for additional light.

Getting into the truck, Roy Jenkins stubbed his rubber boot on something hard and heavy. He reached into the grass and raised up a mold-covered monkey wrench.

Dark spores of luminescent green had spread thickly across the adjustable end.

They placed it carefully in a heavy, clear plastic specimen bag and sealed it tight.

The truck backed up, turned around and went back the way it had come.

While Nathan drove, Frank studied the wrench through the plastic with his flashlight. Was it his imagination, or did the green mass clinging to the metal actually move and change color when he pressed the beam close to the bag?

CHAPTER NINE

When Oral Jarvis had been a guide in the Okefenokee, he had taken adventurous teenagers by boat on overnight camping trips to where Billy Bowlegs, a famous renegade Indian, once had hidden from his white persecutors.

Late at night, after a few good hair-raising stories around the campfire, it was a good bet that Jarvis would spin his favorite yarn. The fact he'd forgotten who'd first told it made absolutely no difference; he embellished the tale each year.

"If you sit here real quiet," he would say, lighting up a stained corncob pipe, "you can hear the swamp breathing." His eyes then would go weird and misty, and every kid would pull his feet in closer to the warm fire.

"'The shadowy people' are out there, you know. 'The shadowy people,'" he repeated with special emphasis.

"All the way from Mexico they once came; many, many years ago, before the Seminoles even. Ate big damn cougars up to 250 pounds and 7 feet long. That's why they's no big cats left around here. Don't see many bears now either, but the bear, he's smarter than the cougar. When a bear hears any people comin', he's quiet like a snake."

He always paused dramatically here, staring at something beyond the dark swamp.

"Now listen, and hear this good. You stay near the campfire, all of you. Cause 'the shadowy people' are lookin' at us right now, and maybe, by God, they're hungry tonight!"

It was night again in the Okefenokee, and the swamp was breathing a hot and fitful breath. A great white horned owl sat in the bare haunches of a dead oak tree, his night-sensitive eyes trained on a small yellow rat snake below. A clown-faced raccoon paused, tense as a statue, sniffing the musk odor of a lurking alligator. A pygmy sunfish, hiding beneath a lily pad, was coolly marked by a giant razor-tooth gar. A cottonmouth lay quietly on the lower limb of an ironwood tree, stalking a click-clicking cricket frog clinging to the bark at the trunk.

Then a shuffling sound was heard along the thin trail edging the swamp, and a strong odor came forth—an all-enveloping odor similar to that of swamp gas. And every animal except the cricket frog locked its muscles and shut its mouth. Now only the frog's steady clicking, like that of a frightened rattlesnake, could be heard along the trail. And the shuffling was louder.

The yellow rat snake slithered through the prairie grass in time to avoid being stepped on by a massive plodding foot.

Other feet followed; like stumps of trees, they thudded against the trembling peat.

In the moonlight, they conjured up a madman's dream, as if the twisted, moldy roots of the cypress bay had come to life to march wearily down a swamp trail for night planting.

Were these "the shadowy people" with which old Jarvis had terrified his campers? These things that walked on two legs? They moved slowly and only at night, as if in controlled dementia, the warning scent from their tumescent skins preceding them.

They numbered over forty, and as the last of their ranks passed through onto the road, it drew back a pawlike hand and smashed the cricket frog for his noisy insolence. Smashed him to red dripping pulp against the bark of the ironwood tree.

This morning Mimi Vandergot felt older than her seventy-five years. She was up twice during the night worrying about Randolph.

The first time, she awakened to a noise in her husband's

library. She had ventured downstairs to discover Randolph pacing back and forth, mumbling to himself. He hadn't seen her, so she simply closed the library door quietly and went back to bed.

The second awakening had been at five-fifteen. A clanging in the street out front had brought her to the window, and she saw a light glowing in front of the hospital. Yes, that would be the search party, she thought sleepily.

For three hours yesterday she had prayed for Sonny's soul. She was deeply troubled by her grandson's disappearance, even more so by the ghastly message left on the recording machine. Might their thriving community be destroyed finally by this horror beyond horrors? Better to die from the bomb than from some sneaky disease dreamed up by deranged men in the War Department.

She hadn't told Randolph yet. Best to let it lie until this afternoon. Until they were sure that Sonny was gone. Really gone.

Mimi removed a skillet from the wood stove and scraped scrambled eggs and leftover hominy onto a Meissen china plate. Pouring an inch of Carnation powdered milk into a large glass, she filled it with tap water. She then poured herself a cup of hot coffee from the pot, and placing everything on a silver serving tray, walked across the dining room into the breakfast nook.

She set down the tray on the oak-leaf table next to a huge leather-bound book that Randolph was reading. Randolph's lips moved with each word; he'd always been a slow reader, despite his advanced IQ. Dyslexia, the doctors called it.

Mimi sat down. Randolph never glanced up.

"Randolph, you've hardly said 'boo' this morning," she said with a practiced grumble.

"Sorry, Mother." Randolph patted the book affectionately. Mimi glanced at the intricate Gothic etchings and the old typeface.

"What is that book?"

Randolph grinned. His eyes glowed with the satisfaction of a cat devouring a canary. "Do you believe in the devil?"

"I thought we'd had enough of the devil." Mimi removed her used linen napkin from its engraved silver ring. "What are you reading?"

"Complete works of Captain John Smith."

83

"I thought he believed in Pocahontas," she said demurely, the charm of a southern coquette still very much intact.

"Don't tease, Mama. When I was ten years old, this was my favorite book in Daddy's library. I read it again last night. Look at these etchings."

Randolph flipped the pages to a particularly ghastly drawing that, fortunately, Mimi really could not see without glasses. Mimi regarded the blur as bothersome and returned to her coffee, adding a half teaspoonful of sugar. "Let's eat first, discuss the devil later, hmm?"

Randolph forced himself to pick up his fork and put hominy in his mouth.

"I don't think you understand the significance of this, Mama. This concerns an Indian devil—Okee by name—the first syllables in the word *Okefenokee*, which means trembling earth."

"Randolph . . ." said Mimi quietly.

But Randolph had already reopened the book to a marker. "And here's a direct quote from Captain John Smith. He says, 'The Indians serve Okee more out of fear than love. They fashion themselves as near to his shape as they can imagine. In their temples they have his evil image carved, painted and covered with skin in such a way as the deformity suits the God.'"

"Extraordinary," said Mimi, sipping her coffee.

"Umm . . ." Randolph put down his fork, leaned back in his chair and for the first time looked out of the breakfast-nook window. He could see three men boarding the yellow Toyota truck. A few other people were gathered around.

Both could hear the truck engine start. The vehicle drove off toward the main gate.

"Your eggs are getting cold, Randolph."

"Yes, Mama, they are," he answered not unkindly. Then: "Mother, do you think they'll find my Sonny?"

There was a long pause.

Mimi had thought that her unused tear ducts had dried up years ago and was surprised to see they hadn't. "No, I don't think so . . ." she said at last.

"I don't either," replied Randolph sadly. "Not today. Not ever."

To the concern of Frank's prickly conscience, the search party this morning had gone off armed to the teeth.

84

No one knew quite what they were arming against, but there was enough evidence to assume that something had, indeed, ambushed Billy and Sonny. Something big and strong enough to drag away their bodies. There also was the muddy footprint Jenkins had photographed at the missile site. It was oversized, slightly webbed and not more than a day old—and not the print of an alligator, as they had thought originally.

"What you're looking at now, Eric, is the wrench-mold sample," said Frank, his voice breathy through the germ filter of his laboratory anticontamination suit. "I spent most of last night separating it from the blood that was underneath."

"Human blood?" queried Eric, still scanning the picture through the viewer of the electronic microscope.

"Testing it now."

Frank put his face mask close to Eric's. "The zoospores, the ones with flagellae, are, I believe, a mutation of scototropic algae."

"Scototropic?" repeated Eric.

"Umm," nodded Frank, his voice sounding tired. "Most plants grow phototropically, or toward light. Scototropics, however, head for the darkest parts of the swamp. And don't ask me why. Science doesn't know that yet. Let's look at the other slide."

Frank pushed another button with his surgically gloved finger, and with a slight whir, a tray ejected slowly from the console. Frank removed the slide, gingerly placing it into a plastic box by itself; the top then was sealed shut. Eric popped open another box, this one marked "X RAY." He put the new specimen into the tray, and Frank adjusted the controls.

"Well, that's unusual," murmured Frank.

"What is?"

"When I X-rayed this slide early this morning most of the spores 'browned' over, and I was sure I'd killed it. But look at this; I've never seen *anything* reproduce this rapidly. I must have stunned it into more activity."

As Eric pressed his faceplate to the viewer, he saw a microscopic community of hydralike spore-bearing creatures literally boiling over each other; their common pigment glowed an oily luminescent green.

"Damn!" cried Eric.

"Quite an aggregation. And that's just a slight dose of radiation."

85

"Are these plant or animal?"

Frank smiled. Eric was a fast learner. The term "aggregation" normally was used with swarms of connected amoebae; and since the amoeba was classified protozoan, it usually was considered to be part of our *animal* ancestry.

"Both or neither. How's that for an answer?" said Frank. "I think what we have here is a kind of primordial soup. I've tried to isolate one species of microorganism from the other, but so far, no luck. They all seem very compatible . . . a world of their own."

"Inner space, huh?"

"Yep . . . that's close enough. What I've been looking at all night is like nothing I've ever seen before. The amoeba is not your *average* cell-splitting type. Instead . . . seems to be a kind of fungoid with many characteristics of an antibiotic mold. It's cryptogenic; could be animal or plant, but . . ." For a moment Frank was lost in thought. "But I want to measure the reproductive cycle of the radiated spores on the computer."

"The amoebae aren't the only organisms in that . . . that soup."

"Right, Eric. There's also a kind of alga, or a slime mold of sorts. Gives the soup its brackish green color. And then, of course, we have the Army's Enteropathica Hominus III, whatever that was . . . or has become."

Frank squinted across the room at the mice in their separate clear plastic boxes. The overhead fluorescent lighting hurt his eyes now. A whine in the generator was getting on his nerves.

"I injected those mice with the wrench sample last night." He looked at his watch. "They've been exposed for over eight hours; should be enough time for any bacteriological-warfare concoction to lay them out. Shall we take a look?"

A moment later they were standing over the mice, who merrily were chasing their tails around and around their plastic prisons.

"Seem healthy," said Eric.

"Don't they," said Frank, checking last night's notes on a clipboard beside the boxes. "Let's get blood samples before I fall asleep on my feet."

Four hours later the blood cultures from the mice had told them absolutely nothing. Evidently the natural defense system in the body of a tiny mouse could more than cope with the strange new microscopic mutations.

86

"We seem rapidly to be approaching a dead end, Eric," said Frank. He was sitting down for the first time in fourteen hours. "I don't even know what we're looking for anymore."

"A clue," said Eric somberly.

"We know we have a real oddball that can multiply itself by the billions in just a few minutes with a light touch of X ray. That's odd, but then under normal conditions a single normal bacterium can multiply in our blood and on our bodies by the millions in just a few hours. It's been said that there are as many creatures on each of us at one time as there are creatures on earth."

"Unto ourselves, we are a universe," said Eric moodily.

"Whose quote is that?"

"Just made it up."

Frank cracked a smile. "That's good, Eric. You sound like Carl Sagan."

"And the blood on the wrench?"

Frank shook his head slowly. "I still can't make up my mind if it's human blood or not. In some ways it is, and in some ways it isn't. Like everything else, its DNA structure has been altered within the past five years."

"But it's cancerous, right?"

"Extremely. Heavy white-cell count; but then they're not normal white blood cells either. They're a rare type nicknamed Medusa, which first was discovered in a leukemia patient at the University of North Carolina just a year before the war."

Frank paused, wishing he had a cup of black coffee.

"The Medusa, an oddball macrophage, one of those piranha-like cells that kill invading bacteria. This one kills . . . or invades other white blood cells. Again, we're looking at Chapter One of a book yet to be written."

Frank stood up slowly, yawned and stretched.

"Like much of science, it's still a mystery, Eric . . . and now I'm going to catch some sleep on the operating table. Wake me up if anyone decides to operate."

"And what shall I do now?" asked Eric, despising the thought of being inactive.

Frank blinked slowly, trying hard to draw a bead on at least one coherent thought.

"Okay, Eric, here's what I want. I'd like you to find out what either slows down the reproductive cycle of those spores, or kills them. While I crash, I want you to find out what 'cides' work best."

"Sides?" asked Eric.

"Fungicides, pesticides, herbicides, antibiotics, arsenic, acids, sulfur . . . try everything in the cupboard." Frank walked toward the door of the operating room.

"Any special order?" Eric was excited again.

"Nope, you're on your own," said Frank, opening the door.

Eric smiled broadly through his faceplate. The door closed. Freedom at last to experiment, he thought. Freedom at last.

Wilkes pulled back on the charging handle of his M-16 rifle. A 5.56-millimeter steel-jacketed bullet hugged the top of the magazine, ready to be slammed into the chamber and fired. Standing in the sun-warmed doorway beneath a broken TV monitor, Wilkes, Nathan and Roy Jenkins prepared to search the underground missile complex.

At the cypress bay, earlier, they had found not a clue. Not even the motorcycle.

After a brief discussion, they had decided to move on, to explore the missile base where Jenkins had discovered his now-famous footprint.

In the truck they had joked about its origins, but now they were edgy. No one relished meeting the owner face to face.

"Who's first?" asked Jenkins.

No one volunteered.

"Guess I am," he said, sucking pure oxygen through his ill-fitting false teeth. "Stay right behind me." He flicked on a waterproof flashlight.

He pushed against the heavy cement bunker door. It groaned open slowly on rusted hinges, and they felt the coolness from far below rush up and flutter against their rubber suits.

Once inside, there were no windows, but they each had a flashlight.

Down a narrow corridor they trooped, rifles at the ready. Past the mildewing sentry's desk, past an upturned metal chair with moldy plastic seat, past the ever-present security monitors until they arrived at a deep well-like, cement-sided hole six feet in diameter.

On the brink they paused, staring fifty feet down a metal ladder into a murky bottom.

"Long way down," observed Jenkins. His bones ached.

Again, no one spoke.

"I'll go first this time," said Nathan, snapping his flashlight to his webbed belt and adjusting the rifle sling taut across his broad back.

"Keep your hands on the sides of the ladder," warned Nathan, "and they won't get stepped on."

They went down slowly.

At twenty-odd feet, Nathan's rubber boot slipped on something. He held on as he swung above the abyss. "Watch your step here!" he yelled, his metallic voice reverberating up and down the hole. "These rungs are slippery with some kind of fungus!"

The last half was harder. The deeper they went, the more slippery the ladder became.

Finally they reached bottom, their feet sinking into two inches of greenish muck.

"Muddy here," exclaimed Nathan, his turn to state the obvious. He aimed his flashlight down a horizontal tunnel.

Breathing hard, Jenkins fell the last few feet. "Too old for this crap," he mumbled, struggling with his gear. Nathan helped him up.

"How much oxygen do we have left?" asked Nathan.

"Maybe three-quarters of an hour," replied Wilkes, rechecking his gauge.

Nathan glanced at the watch on his rubber sleeve. "Fifteen to get down. Shouldn't stay more than ten. Long way up."

"Then let's move," said Wilkes. He was breathing almost normally.

They stopped only briefly at the first tunnel cross section, then decided to continue straight ahead.

Two minutes later they approached the end to the tunnel— a massive open door over a foot and a half thick.

If there's anybody around, this is where they'd be, thought Nathan. He hated the rubber suit and mask. They cut down on your awareness—a kind of sensory deprivation. All you could hear was your own breath. All you could smell was odorless oxygen.

One foot in front of the other, he forced his body forward until he was beside the door.

He flicked his light inside, half expecting to be attacked by a web-footed monster. Nothing moved. It was like a tomb.

Not a tomb exactly, thought Nathan, as he crossed the threshold. Looks exactly like what it is, a command center.

He waved his flashlight across the dry linoleum floor, illuminating empty Coke bottles, cigarette packages, a Hershey bar wrapper, a rotting *Playboy* magazine. Relics for tomorrow's archaeologists, mused Nathan, his light swinging over to the compact control panel with four computer consoles in a row, their screens shattered as if someone had deliberately punched them in. The chairs too had been overturned and looked as though they had been ripped up by a bulldozer. He could still see where they'd been yanked from the deck, bolts and all. Papers scattered everywhere, ripped to pieces, or crushed into balls.

"So this is where we fought the war," said Nathan through his tinny voice box as Jenkins and Bonner approached.

A bank of TV monitoring screens hung over the control panel. They too had been smashed; plenty of glass to cut yourself on.

And as he flicked his flashlight beam down to the shards on the floor, he saw just around the side of the upturned chairs a thoroughly mildewed logbook.

He took one step forward and kneeled to pick it up.

When he pulled the book from behind the chairs, a bony hand came with it.

"Jesus!" he exclaimed, and dropped the book quickly.

"What is it?" yelled Jenkins, his trigger finger twitching.

"Don't know," said Nathan. He moved closer again with his light. "Help me pull these chairs aside."

They lifted the chairs and saw a mummified corpse, flesh dried close to the bone. And though the military uniform had long since rotted away, a few items were intact: the tattered duty belt with its leather pistol holster, a stainless-steel belt buckle, a small pile of change where a pocket should have been, a Timex wristwatch with a metal flex band and a half-open moldy leather wallet.

While Jenkins examined the wallet for identification, Nathan retrieved the logbook.

Slowly opening the flaking cover, he saw that most of the pages had been ripped out.

Wilkes perused the eyeless, mummified head. Something odd here, he thought.

When he pushed at the skull with the muzzle of his M-16, it rolled away from the neck bone. Wilkes leaned down, studying it with his flashlight.

"Know something?" he said after a quick diagnosis. "This guy's got a bullet hole in his head. Right through the fucking temple."

CHAPTER TEN

No one had seen it happen except old Sharptooth.

Scarlett lay frozen in motion in the tall meadow grass, jaw askew. Dim and dead, her eyes stared blankly at the moon, head twisted away from body in a most unnatural way.

Yes, the old alligator had watched, from a distance. And to him, of course, the kill had at first seemed perfectly natural. When you're hungry, you simply reach out and grab something. You pick it up and shake it until the insides snap and break, until the warm blood flows down your throat and the hot flesh satisfies your hunger.

But the bones and flesh still were immaculately dressed in brown and white fur. They had not been eaten. They'd only been left to rot.

The dog's neck had been broken simply because it barked. Simply because its attackers wanted it quiet.

Old Sharptooth plodded through the grass up to Scarlett's rigid body, debating whether or not to drag the cold meat down the hill to his muddy lair.

But instead, the cowering flock of sheep caught his avid attention. They were gathered together nearby and were bleating, and there were no dogs around, no one to protect those sheep tonight.

The cold-eyed predator turned slowly, and pushing the meadow grass before him, stalked silently up the hill.

Inside the church rectory Coleman lanterns cast a harsh, tense light on adult faces—somber men and women sitting around a rough-hewn table.

A knock at the door.

Wilkes got up to answer. Frank eyed the door nervously and finished answering a question.

The door opened.

Disdaining help from Wilkes, Randolph rose stiffly from his wheelchair, and with the aid of his cane, hobbled inside.

"Sorry to be late," he said with a warped smile, "but I fell asleep."

"Glad you're here, Randolph," Frank said quickly. "Please have a seat."

While Randolph settled into a chair, Frank surveyed his notes jotted on a small pad. So far he had described only his own scientific part in the eventuate drama, which, although startling to him as a scientist, no longer threatened to destroy the entire community. Nathan's discovery, however, was something else.

"Let me summarize, then..." said Frank, mainly for Randolph's benefit.

"Since Enteropathica Hominus III no longer is traceable, I don't believe we're in the throes of an epidemic. If the Army's bacteria still were active, our lab mice would most likely be dead."

Frank glanced up at eleven disciples gathered in the stained-glass window over their heads. They were confronting Judas.

"Then there's the blood on Sonny's wrench. We tested it. It's neither Billy's nor Sonny's. It may not even be human. However, it is cancerous in the extreme."

Frank glanced back down at his notes. "Third (and this gets tricky)...we've tested the fungoid material from the wrench, which is primarily a slime mold mutation. Very primal stuff...at least it *was*. But if we're to judge it by its reproductive capacity, I'd say it probably has evolved billions of years ahead of its time. And what's even more extraordinary, since we were unable to destroy it using standard poisons, Eric finally had to zap it with his blowtorch."

Frank could see Randolph doodling, like an inattentive child, on the back of an envelope.

"We injected our lab mice with no tragic results," Frank continued. "For the moment at least, we can assume that whatever it is, it's harmless to mice. That's all from my end. Questions?"

Randolph continued sketching. "You going to find my son?"

Here it comes, thought Frank. I hope the poor guy can take it.

"I don't think so, Randolph."

"You're going to give up looking?"

"We've found no trace of them, Randolph. And we have just enough gasoline in reserve to keep our emergency generators going."

There was a long, painful silence, only the squeak of a felt-tip pen pressing hard against paper.

"I think our efforts are better spent concentrating on our youngsters and keeping to routines," said Frank, wondering what Jesus might recommend in this situation. "We can't spread a small society too thin, particularly with two able bodies already missing. Make sense?"

Randolph's eyes narrowed, and, for an instant, Frank could see a fraction of the mind that used to be Senator Vandergot's.

"If there was strange blood on the wrench," said Randolph, pressing his forehead, "can we assume someone or something was hit?"

Frank was careful; it was time for Nathan's contribution. "That's a reasonable assumption, yes."

"And if there was a fungus, or fungoid as you called it, mixed with the blood, it's possible that whatever was hit, also was covered with the fungus?"

"Entirely possible, yes," said Frank.

"Then, damnit, what type of swamp animal could attack two boys on a motorcycle and carry them both away?"

Randolph's words hung there like a radiation-level alert.

The time has come, thought Frank. Grimly he gestured to Nathan, who was clutching the rotted logbook.

"Nathan?" whispered Frank.

"Roy has something to show us first," said Nathan.

Roy Jenkins removed an eleven-by-fourteen black-and-white enlargement from a manila envelope and passed the enlargement to his left.

"This is one of the footprints I photographed at the missile site. At first we thought it was that of a medium-sized alligator, but . . . we don't know what it belongs to." He paused self-consciously because he'd had too much to drink, then abruptly decided he *had* the right to make a personal assumption.

"No doubt in my mind, though, there are other . . . umm . . . people out there, living in the swamp," Jenkins said quickly. Then he ducked his head to the table and glanced up to Nathan.

Nathan opened the brown-stained logbook. It was encrusted with petrified spider eggs and dotted with wormholes; most of the pages were torn out.

"This is the handwritten diary of an airman named Samuel Wysinski, written two and a half months after the Easter holocaust. He's a poet . . . of sorts."

Nathan sucked in his breath, then dove in.

"'I am the last. The others already have changed their skin. A metamorphosis.'"

Ah . . . thought Randolph as his fingers stiffened around his pen.

"'And I too am changed,'" continued Nathan. "'No longer do I recognize this handwriting as my own.'"

Nathan turned a mottled page that fairly crumbled in his fingers.

"'In fact, I know little of myself. Unclean monster from a netherworld stewing slowly in my own deadly juice. When was I contaminated? Long ago, or was it yesterday? Today, as my watch ticked beneath my new skin, I heard myself scream across millennia:

I am rage.

I am terror.

I am obscene.'"

Randolph's facial muscles began to twitch violently. He put one hand to his face, while his other continued doodling.

"'And the new life began as such things always begin—in the ooze of unnoticed swamps, in the darkness of eclipsed moons. It began with a strangled gasping for air."

The next few paragraphs were indecipherable; then in an awed whisper, Nathan read Wysinski's last will and testament: "'Here in my rotting hand lies cold metal. Here is salvation. Forgive me, dear God.'"

Slowly, Nathan glanced up from the logbook. He was trembling as he'd done each time he read this passage. It was repulsive. Yet, at the same time, it somehow broke his heart.

The pause following Nathan's reading was leaden. The

writer had affected Nathan, and Nathan had affected everyone in the room.

Strange, he thought, the power of a few hand-scribbled words: *I am rage. I am terror. I am obscene.*

"What happened to those missilemen, Frank?" asked Anita, severely shaken.

Jenkins answered first. "This Wysinski was shot in the temple at close range but he was the only one we found." Jenkins twisted the thick Oklahoma University ring on his finger. "A base like that must have had over fifty trained men."

"So they all went somewhere to die," said Anita, her voice slightly hysterical. She turned to her husband. "Can a person live with the type of cancer you described? Can they live with so few red blood cells?"

"I don't know," said Frank defensively. "The white cells dominate almost ten to one, a count similar to those of the victims who died at Hiroshima . . . and recently, every city in America."

Frank stared silently at the logbook in Nathan's hands, then said, "Whatever this man Wysinski means by this diary, I suggest that we not alarm the children by . . . by repeating its . . . poetic substance. I also suggest that, during the day at least, we maintain life as usual on campus. School continues. Everyone's duties remain the same, except that we'll be tired from our late-night watches. Are they any questions?"

Randolph continued to draw while Dr. Alden's last words blurred and faded. Randolph Hollingsworth Vandergot was a child again, resurrecting childhood demons of monstrous shape and nightmarish intensity, his scarred face white, withdrawn.

He did not remember his mother coming to fetch him, to take him to their own private vesper service, which they had held each night for the past five years.

But he did remember her pushing him down the aisle toward the front door of the church. He remembered the chirruping of the crooked wheel on his chair. And most of all, he remembered looking down into the heavy metal heating duct on which his mother had left him briefly while opening the front door. At first he'd seen nothing but two padded steam pipes; then slowly in the dimness, a monstrous face, composed of what seemed to be rubbery lichen, took shape, and he thought he could smell its sulfurous breath.

Wait, Mother! Wait! His mind screamed.

But before he actually spoke, Mimi had rolled him outside. And closed the church door, which, as usual, locked quietly behind them.

CHAPTER ELEVEN

Two figures were silhouetted by the glare of flashlight. One turned the key to the lock of the laboratory door.

Both entered.

One whispered to the other to pull the blackout shades.

The flashlight beamed across white laboratory walls to the sterile table where cultures were kept.

Then the light moved away from the culture boxes to a Coleman lantern.

"Are they closed tight?" whispered Eric.

Velma pulled the last window shade shielding the room against moon and stars.

"We shouldn't be here without permission, Eric."

Eric removed the glass from the Coleman lantern; he fired it with his Zippo lighter.

While Velma Lee watched, he opened the culture box and held the lantern over the individual covered plastic pots inside.

The fungus glowed a most radiant green. Velma, naturally curious, moved closer.

Her voice was half wonder, half reprimand. "Eric, I said . . ."

"Look, I promised Doc I'd find out what kills it."

"Well, he didn't mean for you to sneak up here in the middle of the night." Velma stared nervously at the cultures. "Besides, don't we have to wear those rubber suits?"

Eric rolled his eyes in mock anguish. "Look, Velma, you agreed to come with me, to act as my assistant. I happen to know what I'm doing. I also happen to know that there is something very strange going on. We, the children, are not being told everything. Why the armed guards, for instance?"

Eric began setting out various potions he had prepared for this experiment.

He does look as though he knows what he's doing, thought Velma. But then, he always looks that way.

"Judging by the undercurrent of supposedly adult conversation," continued Eric, "our mutant fungoid here may somehow have caused Sonny Vandergot and Billy Bob Morris to disappear."

"How, for God's sake?" Velma pulled on a pair of surgical rubber gloves that were lying on the table.

"I don't know. But doesn't it strike you as rather peculiar that we can't kill it?"

Good question, thought Velma. She removed a green lab jacket from the nearby wall, watching Eric while she tied it on.

"Eric, what were those pills you took after supper?"

"Pills?" asked Eric, wide-eyed.

"I won't tell. What are they?"

"Something to keep me awake until I finish my work."

"Speed?"

He simply stared at her.

"Oh." She paused. "I thought you seemed different tonight."

Eric stopped arranging the acids and tinctures.

"Look," he said quickly, "this happens to be an emergency. I've been invested with the authority to make this experiment, so if you don't like it, bug off."

"Don't you talk to me that way, Eric Stapleton!"

"Shhh!" he said, grimacing.

"Then don't talk to me that way."

"Okay, okay," he muttered deprecatingly. He puffed air out through his peach-fuzzed cheeks.

For the next four hours they worked together peacefully, Eric treating Velma with the respect she demanded.

Velma looked at her watch. It was two thirty-five in the

morning; the laboratory was hot with all the shades down. She was exhausted, even more so watching Eric work. He never stopped. And though she never would have suspected him of having a real drug problem, she did wonder how long he had been taking amphetamines. Maybe Eric had gotten them from Sonny, she thought. When Sonny worked in the lab, he used to make up all sorts of things.

Poor Sonny, she thought. Poor Sonny and Billy, she corrected, not wanting to show favoritism.

Eric seemed to think they were dead by now; his theory was that they'd been attacked by a mutant horde of killer alligators covered with slime. Eric, of course, loved science fiction.

Well into a new experiment, Eric used a dropper filled with various chemicals and tested it on small bits of fungus samples in rows of glass bowls.

As usual, the fungus would recoil briefly, then bounce back even stronger, changing from green to dullish brown and back again.

"Metachrosis," said Eric. "Like a chameleon changes color by contraction and expansion of chromatophores." He laughed to himself. "Except there's no chameleon."

Eric interrupted his work for five minutes to go to the bathroom. When he returned to the lab, Velma could see that he was all jazzed up again. This time she held her tongue.

"Amazing stuff, just amazing," exclaimed Eric, poking at the specimen with a thin glass pestle. "In my opinion, it secretes some kind of super acid solution that neutralizes anything touching it. Almost like a stomach inside out. But more specifically like the stomach of a termite accidentally imported to Florida that used to eat Florida houses from top to bottom—plaster, creosoted wood, anything."

"Termites?" asked Velma incredulously.

"Yeah. Termites have a perfect symbiotic relationship with the bacteria in their stomach. They're two independent organisms, yet they function as a whole. Fact is, that's the way the termite evolved. The bacteria digest food; the termite's gut provides it a safe home. And one can't survive without the other."

"What are you saying, Eric?"

"Just rambling," said Eric with a manic smile. "But speaking of symbiotic relationships, I'd sure like to know how this stuff survives. It's lichenlike, and lichen itself is half fungus, half alga, adapted to survive under very hostile conditions." Eric

99

paused. "'Adapted,'" he said emphatically. "That's Doc's favorite word, isn't it? Well, Doc thinks that the human cell is evolved from the adaptation of various bacteria that at some point decided to live in harmony—in symbiosis—maybe that's the clue, the key to the successful evolution of a species. Maybe the driving factor of life is not survival of the fittest at all, but symbiosis. And if we use that hypothesis, then the human race is descended, not from monkeys, but from symbiotic or friendly bacteria. How's that for making you feel small, Velma?"

"Umm-hmm," said Velma. Eric was babbling, it seemed.

Eric stared at the fungus, then cocked his head to one side and grinned almost beatifically.

"You know, Velma, there's one thing we haven't tried on our old fungoid yet."

"What's that, Eric?" Velma said warily.

"My hand."

"Don't be an idiot!" she said quickly.

Eric raised his index finger—the "up yours" sign—and frowned.

"Pierre Curie measured the heat given off by radium as 140 calories per gram per hour by burning his own arm. Now, there was a scientist worth his salt." Eric reached for the bowl.

"Don't!" said Velma, too late.

"Now watch it," said Eric. He mixed the fungus around with his finger, then raised it quickly toward Velma's face. "Here, taste this!"

Velma jerked away, frightened. "That's not scientific; that's stupid. Eric! I'm going to get Doc!"

Eric giggled. But the giggle soon turned back to a frown.

"Itches," he said, and brought his finger close to the hot Coleman light.

Like a volcano, the fungus began to bubble over. Within seconds it had doubled and tripled in size, and now it spread over the tip of Eric's finger.

Both Velma and Eric lapsed into shock.

Velma recovered first.

"Well, do something, Eric, it's spreading!"

Eric stood with a frozen finger pointing into the air. He was horrified.

"Do what?"

The fungus multiplied itself even more rapidly now. It spread over half the boy's finger.

"Scrape it off, quick!" cried Velma.

She reached for the Swiss Army knife in her Levi's pocket; she pulled it out and flicked open the blade. "Put your hand on the table."

Eric stared hypnotically at his finger, completely covered now. "This is weird; this really is weird . . ."

Then he caught himself and began to think rationally again. He motioned Velma's hand away. "Don't get near me, Velma. Just do exactly what I say. The only way to kill this stuff is to burn it off."

"You can't burn your . . ."

Eric turned on her. "Look, do what I say, damnit. I got myself into this; I'll get myself out of it!"

The fungus had multiplied halfway across his hand. "Bring me the acetylene torch from the cupboard over there."

"No!"

"Bring it to me, Velma!"

Velma was in tears as she ran across the room to the cupboard.

She tried to open it.

"It's locked!" she cried.

"Well, break it open! Hurry!"

Eric stared at his hand, now almost totally covered.

Velma pried her knife into the lock, jiggled it around. Suddenly the small lock gave way, and the door popped open. She looked frantically across the darkened shelf for the torch.

"I don't see it!"

"It's got to be there. Look! Use your eyes, damnit!"

"There's a big gas can here, that's all!"

"All right!" he screamed through clenched teeth. "Bring that!"

Velma grabbed the can and darted toward Eric.

"What do I do? Oh, God, that stuff's all over . . ."

"Pour the gas into this pan!" Eric shoved the pan across the lab table with his good hand.

Velma obeyed. But almost out of control, she spilled some of the gas over the sides.

"Now get the Zippo lighter from my right pocket."

"I can't!" screamed Velma.

"Get it!" ordered Eric, in near frenzy.

Eric held his hand over his head as Velma rummaged into his corduroy trouser pocket. Finally she extracted the Zippo.

"Give it to me!" cried Eric.

Velma quickly handed Eric the lighter.

Eric placed his fungus-covered hand into the gasoline, and to his own surprise, felt an intense, searing pain followed immediately by muscle spasm. Still, he managed to light the Zippo with his other hand.

He closed his watering eyes, gritted his teeth and slowly brought the flame toward the pan.

Velma stared hard at the pan. Suddenly her eyes flashed and she knocked the Zippo from Eric's fingers.

It fell to the floor, broken.

Eric's eyes flicked open. "What'd you do that for?"

Velma pointed to the pan. Brown slime was floating to the surface. "Look . . ." she said weakly.

Eric looked.

Very carefully, he raised his aching, twitching hand from the gasoline. Though red and slightly swollen, it was relatively "clean."

"Gasoline?" whispered Eric through his tears.

"Gasoline," murmured Velma, nodding.

Eric stared in disbelief at Velma, then back to the pan, from which a thin, acrid vapor was rising.

"The one thing we're running out of," he mumbled shakily. Then he smiled to himself. "Well . . . now we know what this stuff survives on."

"Us," she said with finality as the laboratory door flew open.

"WHO'S IN HERE?" demanded a loud voice.

Eric and Velma watched as the muzzle of an M-16 rifle poked through the darkened doorway.

Roy Jenkins appeared from the shadows; he was almost as startled as they were.

"Velma . . . Eric, what the hell are you doing here?"

CHAPTER TWELVE

At three o'clock in the morning the moon was high and full, a haunting-cool-bright withered sun.

Nathan sat bareback atop Arafat, rifle strapped across his shoulders. Max, his dog, sat on the ground. They both stared at the first row of granite tombstones marked Cosgrove, Jefferies, Vandergot, Jones... all trucked in by Nathan from Waycross, Georgia, over four years ago.

Assembled here were friends, relatives and, of course, the odd nuclear refugees from Savannah and Jacksonville.

The magnolias on his Elizabeth's grave had turned brown since he'd placed them here early this morning. Touch their fragile petals once, thought Nathan, and minutes later they begin to die.

Arafat raised his chiseled head and snorted, pink eyes flaring. Max stood quickly to avoid being kicked.

"Easy," said Nathan, patting his horse's neck. "Easy now."

Arafat had been temperamental all evening, ever since Nathan had begun his twelve-o'clock rounds. Arafat jumped at shadows, balked at holes in the ground, refused to walk by certain trees.

Nathan eased back on Arafat's reins and whispered into his twitching ear.

"Let's run," said Nathan, and he kicked lightly at the horse's flanks.

"Let's run, Arafat!"

Arafat reared up on his hind legs. Man, horse and dog galloped through the night.

A buzzard rose, shrieking from a dead animal carcass hidden in the meadow grass.

Minutes later Nathan heaved Arafat's reins close to his chest, slowing from gallop to trot to walk.

All panting, they stood still beside an overgrown hedge nearly two hundred yards from the doors of the glowing white church.

A faint cloud crossed the moon.

Max took one step toward the hedge and came to a rigid point. He growled into scattered limbs. Hackles rose along his spine. His muzzle flapped at the strange new scent.

Nathan stared down at his dog.

"What's the matter, boy?"

Stiff-legged, Max approached the hedge. Nathan unlimbered his rifle.

A cool wind blew in Nathan's direction. He urged his mount forward.

When just opposite the hedge, the wind gusted, brushing a soft evergreen limb across his face, and Nathan very nearly fired his weapon.

Control yourself, man, he said to himself and tried to smile away his growing anxiety.

Nathan skirted the hedge and came out on the opposite side. Here a sidewalk led up a scenic path toward the church.

A broken sidewalk.

Max paused. He stood trembling in front of the large hole, where the cement had collapsed under its own weight.

Nathan dismounted and approached the hole. Warily he knelt down beside his dog.

"This has been here a while, Max. These are the old heat pipes that run beneath the university—the ones that used to keep us warm."

Max was not impressed with this explanation. He whined at the hole, pawed at it, looked back up at his master.

"Did you see a rabbit go in there?"

Nathan removed the flashlight clipped to his belt and shined it into the hole.

Carefully now, he began to observe that the grass around the fallen sidewalk was freshly bent, walked on by something much larger than a rabbit. Nathan eased forward. He sniffed inside and winced. An oddly familiar odor landed squarely in both nostrils.

"Phew!" he cried and quickly backed off, wondering if their antiquated sewage system had overflowed somewhere down the line.

Max remained motionless. Nathan reached out his hand and smoothed down erect hairs on his dog's back.

"Okay, Max," he said with a sigh, "you stay here, protect my rear. Give me a nice big bark if any more 'rabbits' decide to keep me company."

With that, Nathan lowered himself and his rifle into the opening.

Max sat quivering on the warm sidewalk, his head cocked, listening.

Not a very appetizing tour, thought Nathan as he flashed his light down the first length of tunnel.

The overhead heat pipes were insulated with some kind of white packing, lending the tunnel a striking perspective of depth.

Checking his rear, Nathan saw that there had been a cave-in about fifteen feet back. Good. One end was totally blocked.

He was getting used to the odor now. Like bathing in a sulfur spring, or was it like something else? Something from his childhood, something that now made his skin crawl in anticipation.

He paused, listening. He could hear Max above the hole, whining. Nathan stared at the upper corners of the tunnel . . . at the spider webs. Those he hated. Hated their brushing against his open eyes when he passed through them in the dark. Hated the thought of a black widow fished from an old boot just last week. Hated . . .

But just a minute . . .

He looked again at the intricate webs. Something had recently cleared most of their centers away. Something as tall as himself.

Nathan rechecked the load in the M-16; he unlatched the safety. He moved stealthily, his ears attuned for sound or movement.

Overhead he saw cracks and crannies where rainwater had soaked through. This structure could fall at any time.

What the fuck am I doing in here?

Don't panic, he thought. Slowly he shuffled his boots forward to avoid distracting echoes.

Don't step in that!

He lifted his boot to avoid a slight depression coated with the same type of greenish muck he'd experienced in the missile silo tunnel.

Nathan ducked as rats scurried along the heat pipes just over his head, like fingernails tapping down a long chalkboard.

His nose itched. He scratched it. It itched some more. He sneezed.

"Ker-CHEW!"

He wiped his nose on his dungaree sleeve and waited for the echo to ricochet away.

Then a sound. A different sound. Was it ahead, or behind him? He flicked the light to his rear. Heard it again, and switched the beam forward. For some reason, the light was fading.

Goddamnit, why didn't I put in new batteries?

He was approaching a cross section in the tunnel. The pipes, behind a wealth of dusty spider webs, crisscrossed about fifteen feet ahead.

Nathan paused. Stood still. Was it someone breathing? Was that it?

He held his own breath. He listened hard, tried to send his ears ahead, bend them around the corner, amplify their sensitivity.

But he heard nothing except a dripping; a simple dripping like a leaky midnight faucet that keeps you half awake and too tired to turn it off.

Plop, plop . . . plop, plop . . . plop, plop, plop, plop . . .

Smiling nervously, he aimed the rifle ahead.

The frantic barking was abrupt and jangling.

Nathan's body slipped into primal gear. He spun around like a professional soldier, rifle at the ready, every hair on his body at rigid attention.

"Max!" he bellowed.

The barking became menacing snarls and snaps.

"MAX!" Nathan shined the light behind him.

"MAX! Max! Max!" mimicked the tunnel.

SLOSH! Slosh!

It was not a loud sound, but it sounded loud coming, as it did, from behind him.

Nathan's bowels jerked; his sphincter barely held.

He whirled with his dim flashlight, freezing it onto the shiny, bloated treelike thing standing at the cross section.

Glistening fat paws went up in front of muddy yellow eyes. It lurched toward him.

"What the hell are . . . ?" babbled Nathan, voice high, plaintive with fear.

The flashlight recoiled upward. Nathan pulled the trigger of his M-16. A few rounds whined down the tunnel. Others hit solid meat with a *thunk, thunk, thunk.*

Nathan heard an almost reptilian cry of pain. He flashed the weakening beam onto the trunk, or chest, or whatever it was that was oozing a thick, pinkish liquid through purple-green folds of . . . no, no, no, not flesh. Not live flesh! Something already dead and rotting and coated with slime, like the body of his childhood friend. That was it! Billy Van Patten! Drowned weeks before. Why, he'd fished Billy's huge body from the river. And when he'd poked the skin with an oar to bring it aboard his skiff, the bloated thing had exploded its God-awful stench in his face! Billy Van Patten had exploded!

Nathan turned and ran toward the sound of Max's horrific snarling.

They came lurching up the hill through the Japanese pavilion area. Not quickly, but with definite intention. Moving as shadows move at night. No fragrant warning this time, because the wind was blowing toward the swamp. They were close by before Arafat saw them. With a frantic whinny, he bolted through the open field.

Max had to face them alone.

They spread out when approaching the dog.

Max backed up against the tunnel hole. When the first one reached out to grab him, he slashed its paw. Another pulled at his tail, but Max got a good chunk. The third one backed off briefly, and Max snarled out his challenge to show them he wouldn't be frightened away.

One feinted to snatch Max's tail. When Max turned to attack, another paw caught his neck.

Wriggling like a snake in midair, Max clamped his formidable teeth into the hand that grappled for his windpipe.

But Max was not in charge.

Silhouetted by moonlight, he was swung high in the air, and his body was smashed again and again against the ground.

Finally he could hold on no longer. With a painful grunt his jaws opened, and he stumbled away limping into the bushes, coughing blood.

Keep calm, keep calm, thought Nathan as he approached the opening.

Then Max stopped barking.

Nathan paused. He was twenty yards from the entrance.

The moonlight that fell with a shiver through the ragged hole was abruptly smudged out.

The first oily, dark figure slipped down into the tunnel followed by a second, then a third.

Turning quickly, Nathan trotted back along the passageway. Then he ran faster, carrying the rifle at port arms.

He slipped.

When he regained balance, he saw *it* standing in front of him, arms spread wide—a caricature of a Japanese sumo wrestler.

"Sweet Jesus! Why aren't you dead?" he wailed.

The thing, though motionless, snorted, as if daring Nathan to come forward.

Nathan aimed the rifle at the awesome head and fired two shots.

One yellow eye flicked out. The monster's head recoiled, taking body with it. The thing dropped its rounded shoulders and wagged its massive head back and forth as if trying to understand what had happened. Then it railed with anguished pain, tearing at its face with massive paws.

Nathan heard answering cries coming from behind. He felt the cement vibrations of heavy feet stomping toward him.

He moved forward quickly, cocking back his muscular leg; and with all his weight behind it, he planted a karate kick into the putrid middle of the thing.

It fell. Thank God, it fell!

His stomach queasy from the raw, rotting stink, Nathan tried to ease around the twitching body that now covered most of the tunnel.

Let me get by it, God, he prayed. Don't let me touch it!

The flashlight, a pale glow, was nearly useless.

Nathan stepped over the lubricious mass and pushed away with his back foot.

Almost pushed away.

A paw reached out. It caught his boot and held on.

"SON-OF-A-BITCH! SON-OF-A-BITCH!" cried Nathan frantically.

He raised the butt of his rifle and smashed it down hard into the snarling horror beneath him. Smashed it again and again.

The thing bellowed each time, trying to catch Nathan with its other bloated paw.

Then with a shriek Nathan yanked his foot free of his cowboy boot, dropped his flashlight and pitched headlong down the dark tunnel.

Limping, Max followed along the sidewalk above the heat pipes.

Both were approaching the church.

Nathan fell, touched something soft. When he screamed again, Max whined overhead.

At last Nathan reached a ghost-blue light hovering through an overhead metal grate.

He reached his hands up, locking his fingers into the heavy crisscrossed metal.

I'M BENEATH THE CHURCH! he screamed, though not aloud.

The cement vibrated against his one stockinged foot. They were coming! They were coming!

He heaved at the grate. It didn't move. IT DIDN'T MOVE! He was now insane with terror. He pummeled the grate.

It gave now. Slowly, but it gave. He pushed it up and forced it over, felling it with an ear-shattering CLANG! on the hardwood floor.

THUMP! THUMP! THUMP! The vibrations were heavier now, much closer.

Nathan threw his rifle over first, then lifted himself through the man-sized hole.

He scrambled forward on all fours. He lifted the grate once again. He slammed it back into place.

He grasped the rear of a heavy wooden pew, forced it on top of the grate.

Whimpering now (as Max whimpered outside the church door), Nathan snatched up his M-16 and loped past the pulpit toward the interior door to the rectory.

He turned the thick brass knob. The door opened just wide enough and closed immediately behind him. He felt for the key in the lock. He turned the bolt with a solid snap.

CHAPTER THIRTEEN

At eight-thirty the following morning a healing sun cascaded dappled light through honeysuckle leaves framing Lynne Jenkins's classroom window. Butterflies and bees moved here and there, siphoning the incredibly sweet nectar from the Victrola-shaped flowers. The perfume from these flowers was everywhere.

A yellow jacket buzzed through the classroom, pausing briefly on Velma Lee's desk.

Henry Baldwin sat the next aisle over, his English lit book open to a chapter on Edgar Allan Poe, his mind on the bullfrog in his Windbreaker pocket.

In the two seats behind Velma and Henry sat Nancy and Kirk, writing notes to each other.

"Tin-tin-nab-u-la-tion," said Lynne Jenkins with relished clarity. She finished printing the word on the board and turned to face her class of four.

Everyone except Velma looked up in rapt attention.

"To the tintinnabulation that so musically wells
From the bells, bells, bells, bells,

Bells, bells, bells—
From the jingling and the tinkling of the bells."

Lynne sang in her lyrical voice. She smiled through brilliant red lipstick.

"Now, the word *tintinnabulation* is to my mind one of the most beautiful in the English language . . . and it's totally Edgar Allan Poe's invention. What's this called, Nancy?"

"Onomatopoeia?"

"Yes . . . like 'Ping-Pong' or 'hiss,' it's the formation of a word by using sounds that suggest the object named. And that is spelled . . ."

Again Lynne turned and began her laborious printing.

Meanwhile Henry calmly prepared a slingshot composed of a rubber band and a paper wad. And, as Kirk finished scribbling his love note, he passed it quickly to Nancy, who gave it a fast look.

"YOU GOT NICE PECS, KID!" it read, "SEE YOU AFTER GYM CLASS." It was signed with a fat arrow-pierced heart.

Nancy raised thick eyebrows, batting her lids to give Kirk her especially coy look, when Velma cried out suddenly in pain.

Lynne wheeled expecting God-knows-what; she'd slept badly after last night's briefing, her nerves on thin edge.

"What's the matter, Velma?"

Velma's hand was fastened to her cheek, her blinking eyes watering.

"Nothing," she murmured through clenched teeth.

"Then why are you holding your face, baby?"

"It must have been a bee. Something stung me, but it's all right now, Mother."

Lynne threw Henry a suspicious glance, but, again, he never looked more innocent.

"Better put some baking soda on it, honey," said Lynne to her daughter, "and, if you can, take the stinger out. You're excused."

"I'll survive, Mother. I'm okay."

Then without looking at Henry, Velma pressed a sharp fingernail through page 78 in her lit book.

"I'll get you after class, Henry Baldwin. I swear it," she muttered. "I'll get you in gym class."

* * *

Half an hour later, Nancy stood in front of her bathroom mirror in preparation for gym class. She pulled her "I'm a survivor" T-shirt over full breasts and was quickly greasing an eyeliner pencil across her eyelids when she heard a familiar knock.

She stepped back to gaze at the pictures clipped from movie magazines and pasted around her mirror, then she smiled and pouted directly at her favorite image, the fairest of them all: herself.

"Coming!" she cried and pulled up her gym shorts. Then in a voluptuous parting shot at the mirror, she cooed, "You're too much, darling!"

With that she was gone from the bathroom and leaping into white Adidas tennis shoes. She sat on her soft mattress and tied the laces swiftly. The knocking was louder.

"Comin', honey pie!" she burbled in the sultry voice of a faded movie queen.

Finally, she stood in front of her bedroom mirror and applied a hint of lipstick. She winked confidently at a nude tearout of Marilyn Monroe, turned and skipped over to the door.

She opened it and screamed.

The green head of Dr. Frankenstein's monster intoned through rubber-scarred lips, "I need woman—wife. I very sad alone."

Then the monster, also dressed in gym clothes, advanced on his openmouthed prospect and made slurpy kissing noises.

"I'll kill you, Kirk Cosgrove!" she exclaimed, recovering with heart-thumping vengeance.

Kirk, laughing, yanked the rubber mask from his head and reached out to embrace Nancy. "Well, hurry . . . the kids are waiting!"

He ducked a roundhouse slap at his giggling face and fled across the grassy mall.

Cursing Kirk's back, Nancy Jean Jefferies raced off in hot pursuit.

Velma Lee finished lacing up huge boxing gloves on Henry Baldwin's small hands. They were in the gymnasium, standing on a wide floor mat normally used for tumbling.

"You sure we do boxing today?" asked Henry. "We've never done that before."

"Of course I'm sure, Henry," said Velma. She kneeled and

put on her own scuffed pair of Everlast sparring gloves. "Dance around a bit, warm up."

Henry didn't move. He simply stared down at the huge maroon leather fists that laced up almost to his skinny elbows.

"Now put your dukes up," said Velma, standing.

"They sure are heavy," replied Henry.

"Kirk asked me to get us ready so as not to waste time. Put your guard up like this." She raised her own gloves high, and though thin herself, there was a certain menacing agility in the way she moved.

Henry mimicked her stance badly, his expression uncommonly sheepish.

"I've never seen a real boxing match," he said.

"Well, that's okay, Henry, you can learn from experience." He looked so pathetic with his elbows absurdly akimbo that Velma was about to reconsider. Unfortunately Henry then contrived a memorably smug face.

"Why, Henry Baldwin," exclaimed Velma, "I do declare, you are a most marvelous specimen of incipient manhood."

Henry grinned his peculiar half smile and skipped around twice, nearly stumbling over his feet in delight at the compliment. Velma raised her gloves. She was thirty pounds heavier than Henry, almost eight inches taller. She jabbed tentatively at Henry's face, her glove touching his nose.

"You're not gonna hurt me, are you?" queried Henry, his confidence slipping fast.

Velma smiled sweetly. "Of course not, Henry. Who'd want to hurt a cute little kid like you?"

Then she knocked his gloves aside with her left and smacked his jaw with a roundhouse right.

When Henry recovered, he was not so much hurt as startled.

"You hit hard!" he bleated and started to cry.

"Put your guard up, Henry!" screamed Velma, getting into it.

"Don't you dare!" whined Henry, backing up.

Velma danced in, jabbed Henry twice in the nose and shoved a semihard right to his ear, causing Henry to topple.

"Damn you! Damn you!" exclaimed Henry. Struggling to his feet, he came back to her flailing. "I HATE YOU! I HATE YOU!" he screamed, behind a red windmill of gloves, none of which touched Velma as she nimbly stepped aside and smacked Henry in the neck with a left hook.

Tears streamed down Henry's contorted face as he turned

to face her. He blubbered a frenzy of curses—a constipation of anger saved up for his parents, who'd left him alone in a desolate world.

"I'll kill you! I'LL KILL YOU!" he raved, and charged once again.

This time Velma did not sidestep. She stepped right into the punches, which were now too weak to hurt; then she walloped Henry hard with both her right and left gloves.

Henry fell again, nose bleeding, snot running down over his lips. He fell, kicking the heels of his gym shoes at Velma's knees.

But she simply shoved his feet aside, sat on top of him and pinned his gloves to the mat. "Tell me you're sorry for everything, Henry. Tell me you're sorry and I'll let you up!"

Henry glared up at her. He sucked down a huge ball of snot and then spit. The bloody mess hit Velma on the cheek, in the same spot as the red mark from his paper wad.

"Why, you little . . . !" bellowed Velma, and she began punching Henry's face from side to side with her overstuffed gloves.

Velma's mind was blank with rage when Kirk's powerful arms pinned her, then lifted her from the scrawny chest of her adopted brother.

"Stop it, you hear! What the hell's got into you guys, HUH! What's it all about! HUH?"

Kirk was furious. He picked up Velma and shook her by the arms until she too cried. Nancy helped Henry to his feet and wiped his bloody nose and mouth with a used Kleenex from her pocket.

"You're a mess, Henry!" she exclaimed, trying to avoid getting his blood on her white gym clothes.

"She started it!" wailed Henry.

"Just shut up, Henry," ordered Kirk. "I don't wanta know who started this, or what! I came down here to teach you people gymnastics, and look at you, both of you. God Almighty, Velma, *you* should know better! You're crazy! Plain crazy!" Kirk paused to catch his breath. "Tell him you're sorry, Velma!"

"I'm not sorry; little pest had it coming."

"Say you're sorry, or by God, I'll tell your mother."

"You wouldn't."

"I would."

"Okay, I'm sorry."

"Say it like you mean it."

"I'm really sorry, Henry."

"That doesn't sound very sincere, Velma."

"That's as sincere as I can make it for now, Kirk."

Kirk turned to Henry, whose face was nearly clean.

"Now you tell her."

Henry looked at the mat. "I'm sorry," he muttered inaudibly.

"Louder, Henry, so the birds upstairs can hear you." Kirk pointed up to the sparrows lining the metal rafters.

"Sorry," said Henry, sniffing and looking just beyond Velma.

"Good," said Kirk. "Okay . . ." He had an idea. "Okay, just to show me you're really pals, instead of gym you guys can clean up the chicken cages today."

"That's not fair, Kirk," said Velma.

"Don't care if it's fair or not, you've both got it coming." He paused, looking briefly at Nancy. "If you guys can't get your own shit together, then you can help the chickens get theirs. And when I'm back to inspect in just one hour, those cages better be real clean." Kirk turned to Nancy. "Let's go."

Both Velma and Henry watched until the couple had opened the door to the locker room and closed it behind them.

Velma looked at her watch, then straight at Henry.

"Well, what are you waiting for, runt? Let's get started."

Max lay on the cool flagstones, his nose pressed against the crack beneath the rectory door. He'd been there all night, whining, listening to his master's feverish breathing and waiting to be let in.

He favored his right rear leg whenever he stood. The left was undependably weak and painful. And so he lay curled up, whimpering and licking coagulated blood from his coat throughout the first cool, light hours of morning.

Now two people were approaching across the green mall, and Max thumped his tail anxiously, watching one push the other in a wheelchair.

When their shadows shielded him from the hot morning sun, he looked up into their dark faces and tried to stand but couldn't. Then he grinned through his front teeth, scratching somewhat feebly at the oak door with a front paw.

"Hello, Max," said Mimi Vandergot, bending over him with eyes too weak to see his dilemma. "Your master inside?"

Max banged his tail happily on the flagstone, then shoved

his nose straight at the crack with a resounding whine that became his first yawn of the day. He was tired, hungry and not a little confused.

Mimi's hand grasped the thick wrought-iron handle on the door and pushed it down smartly. It moved scarcely at all. She jiggled it hard, then stood back, sighing, with her hands on her narrow but arthritic hips.

"How strange," she murmured to Randolph. "Nathan must have locked it from the inside...and there's no key for the front door."

There was a noise from within. A footfall, maybe two. Max snuffed hard at the crack, wagging his tail. They all looked expectantly at the heavy door, all waiting to be let in.

Silence. Only Max could hear his master's erratic breath.

"Nathan!" declared Mimi finally. "Are you in there?" She cocked her head to one side, then pleaded, "Nathan, please let us in; we've come to hold a service."

A chair tipped over. Something dragged itself briefly across the floor, then stopped.

Mimi rapped hard on the wood. "Nathan, if you're in there, please let us in!" Again she listened.

Randolph glowered. "What the hell's he doing?"

"I don't know," answered Mimi impatiently. "Nathan, open the door, please!"

Max whined plaintively, paused, then glanced back at the two people.

Suddenly Randolph's eyes blazed with an old savage fire. Knuckles white, he pushed himself up from his wheelchair and swung his metal cane, attacking the portal with six fast, bouncing blows.

"Goddamnit, nigger, open the door!"

"Hush, Randolph!" ordered his mother, turning on her son quick as a pin. "That's no way for a President to talk!"

"I'm sorry," he replied instantly. "I apologize." And with that he withdrew from the real world into another, half expecting the press to be taking notes that would soon be headlines in the *Washington Post*. "I *am* very sorry," he repeated to his mother. "I don't know what came over me."

Anita heard the commotion as she walked through a series of colonnades toward the library. Frank had been asleep when she tiptoed from their room. He'd been working most of the night debriefing Eric, both of them sealed up in the laboratory.

And today the baby was due. And Anita was going to the

117

medical library to finish up her twenty-third book on child care, and to study a government classified folder entitled "Radiation and the Growing Fetus." She would be prepared, no matter how dreadful the consequences. She would face things squarely and deal with them. She would not feel sorry for herself if, God forbid, anything did happen. She was very lucky to have carried the child for this long.

Then the baby kicked her hard; it wrestled with her insides. "Good boy," she said aloud. "Or good girl, whatever you are. You keep poking around and let me know you're all right in there. We're going to take good care of you, don't worry. Don't you worry."

But *she* worried. Should the baby get its antirad shots as soon as it was delivered, or would her own weekly shots suffice to immunize it for the first few days, as Frank seemed to think. There were so many variables to having the first baby since the war. So many variables.

"What's wrong, Mimi?" asked Anita as she approached the rectory. Why were they standing around like this?

Mimi turned, as if surprised to see Anita so close upon them. Her hand fluttered to her thin chest. "I don't know; it appears Nathan has locked himself in." The hand gestured toward the door, and Max whined yet again.

"Why?" asked Anita.

Mimi shrugged.

Anita stepped forward, and for the first time noticed that Max was in pain. She bent over clumsily, then squatted, half expecting her water to burst. She rubbed her slightly swollen fingers through Max's fur and felt dried globules of blood. Max flapped his tail, tried to rise, but his right rear leg slipped out from under him.

"Max is badly hurt, Mimi," Anita said with some astonishment. Then she stood awkwardly and faced the entry.

After a pause, she placed her ear to the wood and heard an almost subliminal movement inside; possibly someone breathing.

"Nathan . . . are you all right?"

There was a brusque stumbling of footsteps toward the door, and Anita instinctively backed away. Then the unmistakable weight of a charging body smacked against hard wood, and pausing briefly, slid to the floor.

Max was no longer docile. He was frantic, hair standing on

end, snarling at the thin crack between flagstone and oak. Anita yanked him back by his leather collar.

"Stop it, Max! Stop it!" Max coughed from the pressure against his throat, and Anita relaxed her grip. "Is your master all right, Max? Is he hurt?"

Max lay down again, his body quivering, his rear leg splayed.

Anita reached into her jacket pocket and extracted a large ring of assorted keys. She held them up to Mimi.

"One of these, if I can remember which, unlocks a door which opens directly into the furnace room, and from there stairs go up to the rectory. I'll have to find the right key, and if the locks aren't too rusty, I should be inside within five minutes."

"You be careful," said Mimi as Anita departed, "Careful, you hear?"

Randolph hunkered low in his wheelchair, fixated on the face he'd seen, or thought he'd seen, the night before beneath the grate in the church nave. Its strong odor had been the unmistakable sulfuric stench of hell, and now it seemed to be coming from beneath the rectory door itself.

CHAPTER FOURTEEN

Nancy squeezed Kirk's hand as they disappeared down the dark stairwell into the near-black hallway of the gymnasium.

Like moths they gravitated through the dimness of the huge locker room toward the slit light from the casement windows in the walls near the ceiling.

They stood in front of their lockers now, and Kirk reached out, grabbing Nancy up in his arms. He lifted her high into the air, squeezing her waist, then slowly touched her feet to the smooth cement floor, his lips caressing the rising nipples beneath her cotton T-shirt.

"Oh, no you don't, monster," protested Nancy. Her fingers dug into his fair skin, but her arms pushed him away. "Not until we have our hot shower."

"A waste of time and water," purred Kirk, kissing a favorite spot beneath her ear.

"K-i-r-k . . . !" she said, drawing the word out to three syllables and ducking her head away.

"Kirk, the water on the roof is solar heated, and the water itself comes gravity-fed from the reservoir. This is my twice-a-week luxury, Kirk Cosgrove, and you aren't going to sweet-talk me out of it." Her eyes narrowed. "So cool it and get us some towels."

Kirk quickly dropped his hands to his sides. "Okay for you, babe," he retorted with a mocking whistle, "just wait till next time. I'll scare the pants off you!"

Then he pivoted with Gene Kelly smoothness toward the hall door whence they had come, did a movie-monster laugh and jigged down the long line of darkening green lockers.

Nancy's bright eyes followed him. "I'm so terrified ...besides, I'm not even wearing any...PANTS, THAT IS! And one of these days I might get pregnant and you'll have to marry me, Kirk!"

But by then he had been swallowed by the sunless hallway. And Nancy, shaking her head, sat down on a long bench to yank off her tennis shoes.

"I'm too mature for Kirk, that's my problem," she stated somewhat dismally as she examined a bothersome corn on her small toe.

The "cage" just ahead of Kirk was illuminated from overhead by a small skylight of wired glass. The cage was of storm fence design, running all the way to the ceiling, and within this enclosure was stored everything from jock straps to gym socks—"H.C.A." stamped on everything in letters bold enough to discourage outright theft from students.

Once upon a time this gymnasium had been the center of Kirk's ambitions, of his coach-father's quest for an Olympic medal-winning son. In fact, the gym had been named after his father, the ex-Marine and Peyton Place-style lover of Nancy's mother, who had been a nurse at the hospital. Small-town liaisons at Harding College were more common than most "respectable" people imagined.

Kirk pulled open the spring door of the twelve-by-twelve cage and entered. It clicked shut behind him. He walked over to an immense pile of towels, pulled one off the top and pocketed a pink bar of Lifebuoy soap from an open bin.

Then Kirk drew back in disgust.

"Jesus, who took a crap in here?" His nose wrinkled. "Rats, maybe." And with that thought he beat a hasty retreat from the cage, all sexual excitement worked up in the past few minutes draining from his loins. He darted back down the hall, leaving the rotten smell behind him, the smell that emanated from a hole in the floor behind the pile of white towels. Insulated heat pipes were visible in the grayness, and around the hole on the

122

cement deck were slimy wet spots. The heavy grate stood against the gray cinderblock wall.

Kirk's mood was never down for long. It peaked once more as he popped his towel against the dark walls, whistling to himself. Popping and dancing down the hallway, his thoughts just naturally returned to Nancy, to her luxurious breasts, the way she tilted her head back at the point of orgasm, biting her lower lip like a wild, succulent berry and smiling with eyes half-closed, her dark brown soft pubic hair—the perfect Afro—coiling in his fingers. As he slipped into her body with the same intensity of . . . of what? Of winning an Atlantic Coast Conference meet or even an Olympic gold medal. Life had its compensations. And for Kirk, sex was not just one of them, it was everything. And he was secretly glad that Sonny and Billy had gone to the beach last Sunday, glad that he had won Nancy, if only by default. Yet somewhere beyond the joy of the pure sexual encounter he could visualize himself secure in a stereotyped log cabin, sitting by a warm fireside, holding a newborn child—Nancy's and his. And her taking the baby from his arms and feeding it from her full, soft mother's breasts.

Umm, good, thought Kirk, and he licked his lips as he turned from the hallway into the cavernous locker room.

Then he stopped cold.

Something moved behind a row of lockers.

Apprehension played briefly across his surprised face, then softened to a knowing smile. He had a pretty good idea what Nancy had in store for him. She certainly wouldn't let the "monster" bit slide by without retaliation. But, then again, he wasn't going to be surprised, either. It was a game of points, and he intended to stay ahead.

Silently he wound his towel into snapping position, and ducking quickly back down the line of lockers, he began to sneak up behind her.

He rounded the long block of lockers, then tiptoed as he reached the very end. His body tensed like an archer about to send an arrow home. He could hear her carefully controlled breathing as he prepared to sting her trim knees.

Then, with a broad Errol Flynn grin, he leaped around the corner and let fly with the snapping tip of his towel.

"GOTCHA!"

Kirk had less than a second to acknowledge his most grievous error. Two large fungoid arms reached out from a thick, oozing trunk of twisted "tree" and literally embraced him in

123

a suffocating hug. Frantically trying to push away, his hands slipped and slid against the slick outer surface, allowing him no leeway, no leverage, nothing to grip, like being sucked headfirst into a muddy sinkhole that promised both death and sudden putrefaction. Deeper he went, fighting for breath, face into the trunk of the thing, while in his mind's eye, curiously, he could see himself sitting on his father's lap, an old book with comic etchings spread out in front of him: Brer Rabbit flailing against the Tarbaby, fist and knee and foot becoming stuck, becoming a part of the very thing he was fighting, until finally he surrendered and passed out from the struggle and accepted the fetid slime (or was it tar?) now crawling down his throat and nostrils.

Nancy had just slipped out of her gym shorts and stood nude and shivering against the coolness of the subterranean room.

"Kirk?" she called out, having just heard him cavorting about somewhere down the line of lockers. She put her hands on her rounded hips. "Hurry up, Kirk, I'm freezing!"

But there was no answer, only a faint shuffling noise. Rubbing the goose pimples on her upper arms, Nancy walked down the line of lockers toward the shower door. She turned the corner and peered at the ends of lockers graduating into dimness.

"Okay for you, Kirk Cosgrove," she said belligerently. "One more trick and you're not getting any for the rest of the month." From this attitude she expected at least a giggle. When none came, she huffed, "Well, maybe I *will* be taking this shower alone!" And she turned on her heel and marched through the swinging door into the large shower room, which was bare except for the twenty stainless-steel shower heads and handles protruding from cement walls.

Just as the door closed behind her, Nancy heard another sound, this time closer. Damn him, she said to herself. Then she whipped open the shower door about six inches as if she might catch Kirk in the act of sneaking up on her.

But there was only gloom beyond.

"I'm not kidding, Kirk, you've scared the life out of me once today. I don't want to play any more sick games. You're just a big, overgrown, spoiled baby with a really crappy sense of humor!" She was upset now. Kirk had ruined her day.

The single upper window hole of the shower door had been boarded over from the outside, so she couldn't see out once she shut the door again. She wanted to lock it, to lock him

124

out, but with this swinging door you couldn't even derive satisfaction from slamming it.

So, instead, with wasteful perversity, she walked down the line of showers, turning on faucet after faucet until the room began to fatten with steam. She stopped at the very last shower, clenched the handle and yanked it to "warm." After a moment of testing the water with her hand, she searched the cement for the odd bit of last week's soap. She found what she was looking for, picked it up and began to lather under her arms. Then she cursed the fact that she'd forgotten to bring her razor from the locker.

At that instant she heard the swing door open and shut somewhere beyond the rising steam. First she tried to ignore it, but when Kirk took too long to giggle, she became uncomfortable again.

"All right, buddy, if you jump out at me with that mask on, I'll wash your you-know-what with so much soap it'll sting for a week!"

Not a bad put-down, she thought. That should bring him out of hiding. But still there was no laugh from Kirk. Only feet shuffling toward her.

"Don't you dare, Kirk, don't you dare!"

From the corner of her eye she could see the barest outline of a figure coming at her through the steam. The head had a greenish tint. Nancy jerked her head around, refusing to look.

"Take off that mask, Kirk! Take it off, you hear me! I'm not going to look at you!"

As the twisted thing came closer, solidifying from the steam, Nancy angrily began washing her hair.

"I'm going to ignore you, Kirk. I'm just going to ignore you!"

The thing stood only a few feet away and even seemed quite puzzled when Nancy began to sing her favorite Beatle song at the top of her lungs. Finally, with something more than curiosity aroused, it stretched out its pawlike hand and laid it gently on her shoulder.

Nancy lifted both shoulders in total disgust. Her singing stopped.

"Uggh! What is that, you bastard, raw chicken liver?"

Then, of course, she turned to see Kirk. And her face froze in abject horror, eyes bulging too wide for her slender throat to scream.

* * *

The chained padlock on the twin cellar storm doors *was* rusty, but fortunately for Anita, it snapped open with little manipulation. Awkwardly, she lifted one door, and suddenly unable to control its weight, let it fall on its side with a deafening clang.

Coal dust arose from the black entranceway, revealing five sooty cement stairs leading into the bowels of the church.

Anita picked up her maternity skirt and walked carefully down the stairs. Stopping at the bottom, she let her eyes adjust to a dimness, broken only by the shaft of diffused morning light trailing behind her.

"Now, where can the rectory stairs be?" she asked herself aloud, her large green eyes following the line of heat pipes that ran the length of the furnace room.

The huge black furnace, converted to oil in the fifties, then back to coal in the fall of 1980, squatted toadlike in the shadows.

There were no windows here, and the bare overhead bulb with its hanging string looked quite sad and useless. Anita eased forward cautiously. The sun ducked behind a passing cloud, and charcoal grayness settled around her at the center of the room.

Oh, why didn't I bring a decent light? she thought, fishing into her jacket pocket for the small wooden matchbox she usually carried.

The box held three safety matches.

Anita clucked her tongue for her own lack of foresight. Better not use these now, she thought. Might need them on the stairs.

Slowly she made her way to the right of the ugly furnace, where shadows were deepest. She stretched out her hand searching for the door, but felt nothing. She sidled forward another two paces, and her sandaled foot sideswiped something metallic.

"Ouch!" she cried, anticipating pain before actually feeling it. A coal shovel clattered to the damp cement floor, just missing her bare toes. She paused, then stepped over the wooden handle.

Her eyes were adjusting. Before her was the vague outline of a wooden door, the dull glow of a round doorknob. She touched the roundness with her fingertips, then grasped it firmly and pulled. The knob came off in her hand.

"Damnit."

With some effort she stuffed the stem of the knob back into its square hole. She turned it and pulled gently at the same time.

The door swung wide on creaking hinges. In the gaping maw behind the door there was absolute blackness.

"Matches," she said somewhat dismally, and lit the first one, holding it out before her like a poor man's torch. It flickered brightly. Yes, she was in the right place. She ascended the first four stairs, wiping dusty cobwebs from her path.

The match burned out. Save the next two, she advised, then, in pitch black, used her right hand as a guide—palm flat against a wall of flaking paint.

Up she went, step by step, twelve in all, until she arrived at the top.

Her sensitized hand quickly found the doorknob and turned it.

Locked. Of course. She pulled out her box of matches again, then her keys.

Fifteen assorted keys on the ring, only two more matches. She settled in now, getting her props ready.

Something moved downstairs. In the dark she cocked her head.

"Yes?" she inquired, match in hand, and the huskiness of her own voice surprised her.

But there was no answer. Anita shrugged, then struck the second match on the edge of the small box. She looked from the lock to the keys, trying quickly to pair them.

This one, she thought. She plugged the key in, turned it.

Nope, not that one. The match was consumed. One more try.

In blackness again, she could smell something disagreeable. Something rancid. Possibly it was sulfur from the match, but for some reason Limburger cheese came to mind.

The last match flared. She pressed a thick iron key into the old lock.

As she turned the key, the door opened quietly. Inside, light from the stained-glass window cooked the rectory in liquid colors. The shadows were bold, theatrical. Judas reared back from his inquisitors, eyes rolling in surprise. The round meeting table sat like a sturdy four-legged mushroom, a brass processional cross gleamed from its resting place on the far wall.

Anita stepped across the portal and shook out the last match.

"Nathan . . . ?"

A groan came from behind her. Startled, she turned to see Nathan slumped in the only bare corner of the room, head down between his knees.

"Nathan, are you hurt?"

There was no answer. His breathing was congested, erratic. Anita walked slowly toward him.

"What's the matter, Nathan?" asked Anita, all maternal, all concern.

But Nathan refused to look up, and worse yet, seemed to be crying inwardly, to be whimpering.

Anita was much closer now. Her heart radiated sympathy as she knelt before him and reached out a consoling hand to touch his.

She drew her hand back quickly, for, from his fingers up to his elbows, he wore an icing of slippery, translucent mold.

Anita rose quickly to her feet and backed away with an unsteady step.

"Nathan . . . ?" she quaked.

Nathan's glazed head popped up with a moan—a deformed Jack from his box.

Anita shrieked. Most of the man's unusually handsome face was a culture of budding fungi—shining bloody pink in this unholy light.

Anita stumbled backward, nearly tripping, catching herself on the back of a wooden chair.

Nathan snarled deep within, bent over on all fours and began to crawl like an angry, begging leper.

Stupefied, Anita reached behind her. The door! Dear God, where is the door?

Finally she touched it. She turned swiftly to undo the bolt, to be safely outside in the sunny mall.

But the bolt was frozen, impossibly jammed. Hadn't been locked in years. There'd been no need.

Nathan drew closer, slobbering, his body actually leaving behind him a trail of slime. Like a giant garden slug.

Anita heaved at the long bolt with all her being. It inched forward.

Nathan groped a festering hand toward Anita's bare ankle. The bolt slid open.

Anita leaned on the metal handle and the door gaped wide, white light blasting in like a plasmic sunspot while Max barked fiercely and Mimi and Randolph cringed at the sight of the wailing black man with green-pocked arms crossed in front of sunstruck eyes.

Anita ducked outside. She clutched the edge of the door and slammed it shut with all her might—more might than she realized she had. And as the door hit Nathan lurching forward, his body struck hard against wood instead of the warm human flesh he desired.

"My God!" cried Anita, hand to her face, staring unbelievingly at the closed rectory door. She heard the weight of the body inside collapse and slide in a heap to the floor.

"Black Satan!" shrieked Randolph, struggling spastically from his wheelchair, his hand holding high a black family Bible—his only defense.

Max's hackles stood straight up as he barked. Then his back right leg gave way and he began to whine in serious pain.

And as Anita bent down to help the dog, she also could hear sobs of frustration from behind the door and the faint cheeselike odor of something just beginning to decay.

CHAPTER FIFTEEN

The large yellow plastic bucket was brimful of chicken drop-
pings, and the birds themselves, except for one ornery Bantam
rooster, were once again imprisoned in wire cages.

The Bantam glared victoriously at Henry from atop a ten-
foot-high stack of baled hay. Velma finished sweeping a last
bit of dirt into a large green dustpan, then looked at her wristwatch.

"So much for class. I'm leaving."

Henry dropped the broom he was poking the rooster with
and turned. "We can't leave until Kirk tells us."

"Well, it's time to go," said Velma. "I know what they're
doing down there, anyway," she added in a moral tone remi-
niscent of her mother's.

"What?" asked Henry.

"Screwing," said Velma flatly.

Henry actually let out a squeak; he had never heard Velma
talk like this before. "Really?"

"Yeah," said Velma. "When they come up for air, tell them
I've gone to math class. Or are you coming with me?"

"I gotta get this rooster in first," said Henry too quickly.

"Suit yourself," said Velma. She picked up her book bag

and walked toward the gym doors, and Henry just stood there with his mouth open until one of the doors shut behind her. Then he moseyed over to the hay and stuck his hand between a couple of bales near the floor.

Out came a dog-eared collection of *Playboy* centerfolds, and Henry flipped through them in abject concentration until the rooster above him let fly with a virile cock-a-doodle-doo.

Whereupon Henry jumped as if caught in the act and quickly returned the centerfolds to their hiding place. He grinned sheepishly at the rooster, debated for just one second and headed toward the locker room doors.

As Henry tiptoed down the dark stairs, he listened carefully for any sign that Kirk and Nancy might be approaching. He'd watched them making love before, and the sights and sounds had set off all sorts of alarms in his prepubescent glands. Since then he'd become obsessed with sex, like everything else, and if he couldn't have it, he felt he was most certainly entitled to observe it. As long as he didn't get caught. That was Henry's golden rule.

Henry walked like an Indian tracking deer. In deathly silence he peeked around the corner of the hall doorway. Beyond was the locker room—rows of green metal stingily illuminated at the far end by casements near the ceiling.

Henry darted into the room, and ducking from locker to locker, finally arrived at the last row. He stared carefully around the edge.

Toward the end of the long row he could see clothes piled on one of the metal benches, Nancy's running shoes on the floor. If he were caught, he'd say simply that he had to rush to the toilet, which was just beyond the shower room, that he had diarrhea.

Henry walked slowly down the aisle, stopped at the pile of Nancy's clothes, picked up her pair of white nylon shorts and sniffed them. His nose wrinkled in distaste. He dropped the pants quickly and continued toward the shower-room door.

Just in front of the door he paused. Noisy in there. Sounded like all the showers were going at once. Cautiously, he pushed the swinging door open and aimed one curious blue eye through the crack.

Steam clouded the room, but most of it had now risen to the ceiling as the solar-heated water cooled. At the dark end of the shower room Henry could barely see two figures just below the waist. He could make out Nancy's bare legs, the curve of her buttocks and . . .

And what? he thought angrily. Whatever it was, it wasn't very sexy. It wasn't even appealing. Besides, it smelled bad. Horrible, in fact.

Then Nancy's legs disappeared into the rising steam. What was happening? Had Kirk picked her up? Were they coming toward the door?

Henry got ready to run. The crack in the door narrowed to a sliver.

Then he saw *it* coming through the thin clouds of steam. Huge, bloated, green and brown and purple—oily colors like a rainbow on a patch of greasy water. It came; it padded slowly toward the shower-room door, and it was holding Nancy's body over its shoulder like a white rag doll.

Henry's blue eye refused to blink. It absorbed directly, and in the act of absorbing, overloaded his highly evolved computer. What was left—the older, more primal part of his brain—short-circuited an instinct to flee. A stripped-bare wire of alternating terror banged back and forth inside his skull.

The thing was halfway across the room before Henry thought he saw his dead mother Muriel's wrinkled hand wrench his frozen one from the door and spin him around. "Run!" she warned. "Run, Henry!"

Henry ran, but not far, for he was thinking clearly again. He would never make it down the line of lockers before the thing came through the shower-room door. And there might be another one in the hallway.

Nancy's locker door was open. He hopped inside and pulled the metal door almost closed just as he heard the shower-room door swing open.

Closing his mouth, he forced himself to breathe slowly through his nose. The footsteps were louder now. They seemed to slap at the cement as they approached the locker.

Did they pause just outside the locker? Henry thought they did. All he could see through the thin slats in the green metal were the feet of the thing. Yes, it paused a second, and maybe it was sniffing the air, trying to smell the fear leaking from Henry's armpits and dripping all the way down his thin body into his sweat socks.

But it moved on. Perhaps it was confused. Perhaps it had what it wanted. O God, thought Henry, don't let it eat me too!

Henry waited the longest wait of his life. Was it gone now?

All gone? He pushed open the door in time to see *it* and Nancy disappear into the darkness at the other end of the room.

Henry stepped noiselessly from the locker, his eyes and brain alert, ticking. He carefully peeped around the corner of the end locker and his young eyes discerned the faintest outline of the hallway exit. He made a fast mental note of his escape route, then ran. Ran like a March wind, ran like a suicidal ghost fleeing its dying body, ran like sunlight through winter ice. Through the hallway, up the first flight of stairs, through the first double doors, up more stairs, crashing through the interior gym door, where the rooster squawked and flew from his path. Then through the main gymnasium door and outside: Paul Revere riding to warn everyone that the British were coming! No, not the British, the monsters! The monsters! The end of the world was at hand!

Henry raced down the sidewalk through the mall, across the vegetable garden trampling beans, asparagus, Brussels sprouts. Past the scarecrow, past General Lee and his pigeon-shit white hair, past the dry-rotting columns of the old Vandergot house.

"What's happening?" called Mimi from her porch. She was just now recovering from the ordeal at the rectory.

"Doc . . . *where's Doc?*" screamed Henry.

"At the hospital with Nathan, Henry. What's the matter?"

But Henry was too frightened to explain to the old woman. He needed Doc.

"Has everyone gone mad?" called Mimi after the boy. Then she felt her own pulse quicken. Things were rushing along quickly now, much too quickly. If Nathan had some sort of strange disease, a kind of advanced leprosy, then soon—too soon they all might be infected.

Mimi turned back to the open door behind her. "Randolph," she exclaimed, louder than intended, "what are you doing in there?"

Randolph was sitting at the dining-room table, his back to his mother, a small box of .38-caliber cartridges in front of him. He loaded the last round into the revolving drum of his pistol, snapped the mechanism home quietly, then hid the weapon in his lap.

"Nothing, Mama . . . nothing. I'll be right out."

Frank and Eric strode quickly down the hospital hallway, Wilkes and Roy Jenkins close behind them, all wearing anti-contamination suits. Nathan was on a gurney. Except for a small breathing hole and a puncture for the IV tube, Nathan was totally wrapped in a clear plastic body bag.

Nathan had given them a good fight. He had managed to knock two of the men down before Wilkes had tripped him up and Frank jammed his neck with a horse-size dose of Demerol. Even then they'd had to struggle to strap his arms and legs to the stretcher.

Frank directed the stretcher bearers into the emergency room and motioned to the operating table.

"Lay him out there. If he comes to again, give him another dose. We'll relieve you in a minute."

Frank looked through a large observation window. He could see Anita, Velma, and Lynne Jenkins holding Max on a coffee table. Frank tapped the window. Anita looked up. Frank placed his plastic face mask against the thick safety glass.

"Anita, can you hear me?"

Anita shook her head and came closer. Frank waited till they both were touching the glass.

"Tell everyone to stay put in here until I know what we're dealing with."

Anita nodded this time. "Good luck," she mouthed, but Frank already had turned his attention back to Nathan.

Panting, eyes glazed, nostrils flared, Henry looked both ways, up and down the hallway trying to make up his hyperactive mind where Doc might be. Then his eyes caught the "EMERGENCY" sign with an arrow pointing right, and he took off down the long, green corridor.

"I don't think it's broken. Needs a cast, though," said Anita, removing the hypodermic needle from the hairy folds of skin in Max's neck. Lynne Jenkins, assisted by Velma, was holding Max on an improvised operating table. As the dog went limp, his tongue lolled from his mouth. "VELMA!" called Anita.

"Yes?" said Velma, jumping. Through the observation window she could see the men in their weird suits stripping the plastic from Nathan's body. She could see Nathan's skin, blotched with jellied, translucent green. She could hear him moaning as he fought against the taut restraints of the operating table.

"Velma," said Anita forcefully, "concentrate on what we're doing here. Will you get the plaster from . . ."

The door to the observation room flew open. Henry tumbled through, his mouth working. "Doc! Where's Doc?"

Anita nodded toward the operating-room window. "In there. What's wrong with you, Henry?"

Henry pivoted, took two steps and reached for the door handle. Anita grabbed him by the arm, spun him around. "You can't go in there, Henry! Tell me what's wrong!"

Henry's face blanched. "Monster!" he wailed. "I saw a monster grab Nancy!"

"Where, Henry?"

"In the showers! In the gym!"

Anita drew the shaking boy to her. "Calm down...calm down now..."

Lynne came to Henry. Frightened herself, she kneeled, cupped his damp face in her hands. "What kind of monster, Henry?"

"Horrible...fat...just horrible!" Henry threw his arms around Lynne, clutched her by the dress, tried to hide his small, sobbing face in the soft folds of her bosom.

Just then as the drab-suited men in the observation window sprayed their gasoline, Nathan shrieked with rage. And everyone from the next room stared in horrified astonishment as the body of the black man dissolved into clouds of white smoke.

CHAPTER SIXTEEN

The church bell bonged out a distant warning.

A large, muscular hand flicked to the last digit of a combination lock and yanked it loose from a steel door hasp. Stenciled in black on the metal door was "ARMORY/AROTC."

Wilkes threw open the heavy door and stalked inside. He still was wearing his rubber suit, but with the mask off and the headpiece hanging about his neck like a green, hooded sweat shirt. And though he was hot and angry, he finally knew what he was about. After five years, all the liberal college bullshit had boiled down to one thing: You fucking-a-well defend yourself, or you don't—a basic rule on any playground. War he understood.

Wilkes removed the long metal bar that locked row upon row of M-16 rifles. His primary job five years ago had been supervising the armory and occasionally showing would-be Army lieutenants how to take apart rifles blindfolded and put them back together again. And all these weapons still were in damn good shape after five years. He'd seen to that. They'd been to Vietnam and back, some of them, and you never knew when you might use them again. If the Russians *had* landed in Georgia, they wouldn't have marched through like Sherman. A few good men holed up in the swamp could take on an army.

Wilkes grabbed a rifle and tossed it to Roy Jenkins, who also was clad in rubber. Kneeling down beside an ammo box, Wilkes flipped open the lid and began stuffing a rubber pocket full of magazines prefilled with armor-piercing bullets. Roy did the same, but with less enthusiasm. Wilkes glanced at his watch.

"When do we meet Doc?"

"Three-thirty," answered Roy, pulling back on the charging handle of his rifle and inserting the black magazine. "And Doc wants all the pressure spray cans in the gym filled with gasoline."

"What we need is a goddamn flamethrower," said Wilkes. The flamethrower had been Wilkes's weapon in Korea.

On the Naktong line above Taegu, to be exact. Very effective weapon against bunkers and for stopping an enemy charge at night. Wilkes had used it for both. He'd fried at least fifty North Koreans at Naktong. The gooks had his regiment on the run. His reinforced platoon's mission was to act as rear guard while the rest of the battalion slipped away at night. They had waited in a foggy rain, taking direct hits from gook mortars and artillery. Then three hours before dawn the little bastards had attacked in mass, balls out, straight up the middle. Private Jaynes and Corporal Topolski lay to the right of him with their heads blown off from a giant mortar round. Wilkes himself had lost the use of his legs, and since there was no question of running, when the gooks did come screaming through the lines, they had to gargle liquid gas and stack up their black bodies like cordwood. When the dawn finally came, the perimeter was intact. Then some daredevil corpsman managed to put Wilkes and two other GI's in a Jeep and drive out with shrapnel bursting all around the vehicle. A week later Wilkes was in a California VA hospital. Six months later, he was a veteran with a Silver Star, a Purple Heart and two crutches. He left the Army for two years, tried to make it in civilian life. Failed. Reupped, and landed a job with the Army ROTC at Harding College, remaining here through Vietnam and retirement. For the past ten years he had been a janitor.

"What we don't need is another war," said Roy.

"We better be ready," said Wilkes, strapping a K-bar to his right ankle.

"We were too ready for the last one. That's one reason

138

we're in this damn mess," said Roy, his voice dead flat with anxiety.

Just then Roy realized that the church bell had stopped ringing. He crossed himself.

"Let's get up to the gym. If you're still lookin' for action, Wilkes, I guess that's where it'll be."

These last words Roy said with foreboding. And as they walked from the armory, he pulled a silver flask from his rubber pocket, took a stiff drink and passed it to his partner.

Rubberclad, Frank stood in the improvised decontamination shower with his arms raised. Eric sprayed him first with gasoline, then, to be safe, with antibacterial detergent.

Both man and boy stepped from the shower room still buttoned up in their special suits. Frank pulled off his mask and flopped it down on one of the bathroom sinks. Two bottles of Coke stood on the stainless-steel counter beneath the wide bathroom mirror. To the left of the bottles was a loaded Army .45 automatic; ten feet beyond stood Anita, arms crossed over her swollen belly.

Frank licked his dry lips, reached for the Coca-Cola and drained most of the bottle.

"Two more here if you want them, Frank," said Anita. "How's Nathan?"

Frank picked up a towel and wiped away the perspiration stinging his eyes. "Light burns, severe shock, fever."

"That stuff on his skin . . . ?"

"Yes," interrupted Frank, "the same as on the wrench."

"Which means?"

"I wish I knew. What time is it?"

Anita glanced at her watch. "Three-ten. Will you rest a few minutes before you go?"

"Anita?"

"Yes?"

"Round everyone up, tell them I think we all should spend tonight locked in the hospital. Try not to panic anybody."

Anita hugged the baby beneath her arms.

"You be careful, Frank."

Frank removed the automatic from the shelf and slid it into his webbed belt.

"Yeah."

He left quickly.

139

Anita stared at the bathroom door a long moment, ignoring Eric, who seemed embarrassed to be standing there.

"Rather ironic," she said finally.

"What is?"

Anita focused on the ceiling, on the winking fluorescent lights working half strength off the portable generator.

"We have such a lovely fascination for war and horror." She smiled without joy. "It's our fondest nightmare come true, right, Eric?"

Eric opened his mouth to say something, but closed it again when he saw that Anita was about to cry. He watched almost curiously as her fingertips touched her face. And he heard her make the same quiet choking sound his mother used to make so many years ago.

Then with no warning at all, his eyes, too, were hot and full . . . remembering.

CHAPTER SEVENTEEN

Frank had experimented with hallucinogenics during his early twenties at the University of Virginia. On a fine spring evening, he and two other premed students—one a personal disciple of Timothy Leary—had taken 250 micrograms of LSD each, to plumb the collective unconscious, to see what "really" was happening down there.

Their preparation had been a thorough reading of *The Tibetan Book of the Dead*, the abridged Alpert version. This, with the acid, was enough to take them on the same psychic trip Tibetan monks meditated most of their adult lives to experience.

Frank and his friends would use the Russian roulette or, as some wag called it, the "fast food" approach toward understanding the universe. Why spend half your Western life learning what life is all about when you can perceive it totally in one blinding flash? A coated sugar cube was all it took.

And so they tripped.

Gurued by Jim Watkins, they lay on the ocean-blue carpet in a bedroom of the ΔKE house, gripping photographs of relatives like life preservers on a sea that just might get too rough.

All had gone well for Frank. Only one hitch when he saw

his mother's and father's faces decompose from the snapshot in his cold, pulsing hand, but that was okay. "Hey, Mr. Tambourine Man, play a song for me..." Hey, wasn't that Bobby Dylan singing somewhere in the background?

Probably Jim's choice. But Dylan's voice had faded as the acid selected scattered microfilm from seldom-used parts of his brain and Frank felt his body evolve in reverse, whirling back through time, back through the dawn of man—then past man, until he himself was a small, spineless grub worming slowly through primordial mud. Then some particle of his being encountered another force moving incredibly fast, reeling his mind and body forward through time. To the here and now, lying on the rug in the ΔKE house. Then came the realization that this was the end of the line. This was death, and metaphorical or otherwise, it sure seemed like the real thing.

The Tibetans relished it. To them this moment was the dawn of consciousness.

But, damnit, you *had* to die first to allow yourself the experience, to get this behind you. To open your soul to the stars. So Frank took a deep breath and let go. Let something leave his body and float up to the stars, become one again with their light. To become dust. And yes, it was a blinding flash just like Alpert said it would be. And Frank was sated all the next day and for the week beyond, writing poetry and thinking in a way different from before. More curious about the unconscious world. More curious and uncertain about himself.

Years later, he would think over this experience as though he had witnessed a kind of master plan for the human race. Strangely, it had given him some hope for the future—a religious faith in mankind that would not be shaken even by nuclear holocaust. In some way, he was sure he had a special mission to fulfill, and like the prophets of old, he girded up his loins for the good fight.

Jim—what happened to him? Oh, yes, he went on to become a heroin junkie. Ken, a good brain surgeon. Everyone had been affected differently. But it was the start of Frank's true religion. He did believe in a new kind of life force, a renewal. Something. He was no longer afraid of the stars.

And now they were pumping taut the pneumatic handles on the fat, galvanized spray cans filled with gasoline. Dressed like men from another planet, preparing to face down their unknown adversaries and bring back two of their own kind.

War.

Against whom?

Were the enemy conscious beings? Could their fungoid coat infect minds as well as bodies, like disease can affect the mind, like a high fever or cancer can destroy healthy brain cells? Could this be man's ultimate legacy to the world, to become compatible with one of earth's lowest forms of life?

Excuse me, but was not the world a conscious place only because man had been here to observe it, to marvel at its beauty, to unite in its praise with his poetry?

But . . .

If we are humbled by the Darwinian belief that we're descended from monkeys, how do we feel when science confronts us with the possibility that we could actually be descended from two dissimilar bacteria that one day decided to get together to form the first animal cell?

They were walking down the gym stairs, inhaling pure oxygen and darkness, opening the door on a new/old life form.

And who's to say that we are better off than they? thought Frank. Nature has obviously given them a temporary seal of approval.

They have survived for five long, hard years without benefit of the super-protein derivative we've had to take weekly.

The three men stopped in the blackness at the foot of the stairs, weapons clicking against the buckles or snaps of their unwieldy clothing.

Warily, they trooped through the hallway until they came upon the open doorway leading into the locker room, where casement windows at the far end squinted a dull light.

Moving forward now, slowly, cautiously, hoping to flush God-knows-what from its hiding place. Hoping to take Nancy and Kirk safely home.

At the shower-room door they stopped again, looked behind them, worried about their masks, which were fogging in the dampness, obscuring peripheral vision.

They could hear a force of water pounding against the floor inside, and they were afraid.

Frank pushed open the swinging door with his gloved hand; Wilkes slid an M-16 through the opening.

There was no steam. The shower water had long since turned cold. Cold water against cold cement.

The three men stepped inside. The door swung shut behind them.

Wilkes lowered the muzzle of his M-16 to keep the barrel

dry; he and Roy Jenkins went down the line of shower handles, turning them off. Then?

Silence. Just forward of the last shower, Frank discovered a patch of greenish mold. Aiming the nozzle of his spray gun, he fired. A faint white smoke arose. Frank turned his Plexiglas beak from side to side, searching. But there was nothing more to see in the shower room.

"We'll cover the entire building," he declared.

Wilkes and Roy Jenkins nodded. Roy preceded the group back to the shower-room door. He opened it and stepped through.

Without warning, a large fungoid arm grabbed him and yanked him away, screaming. The door swung shut in Frank's face. Instinctively, both Frank and Wilkes fell back; it was seconds before they raised their weapons with the courage to kill.

"Christ Almighty!" exclaimed Wilkes.

"Jenkins! Jenkins!" called Frank. Then he paused and looked over to Wilkes. "Let's get him!"

Wilkes motioned Frank back. He bounded forward and smashed open the boarded window in the swinging door. The splintered wood fell to the floor on the other side.

"Jenkins!" called Wilkes through the opening. "Jenkins! Jenkins! Jenkins!" echoed throughout the cavernous locker room. Wilkes could see nothing. He turned his beak-mask briefly to Frank.

"Watch out!" yelled Frank.

Wilkes ducked. The paw that came grappling through the small window bumped across the top of his rubberized skull, then disappeared again.

"You son-of-a-bitch!" yelled Wilkes. He recovered quickly this time, took two steps back from the door and riddled it with high-velocity bullets that shattered half the thick wood on impact.

Wilkes charged through, Frank right behind him, both looking about and frantically waving their weapons.

The remains of the swinging door flapped shut behind them. Swish. Swish. Swish.

Nothing.

"Damnit!" cursed Frank, seeing only row upon row of gray-green standing lockers.

"Where'd they go?" growled Wilkes.

"Can't be far, damnit!"

144

Frank gestured toward the locker rows ahead. With hesitant steps, they made their move.

They passed the first row. Nothing.

They passed the second row. Nothing.

They turned down the third aisle, headed toward the black hole of the locker-room entrance.

They paused uneasily.

There was a groan of straining metal. Wilkes flicked on his flashlight. The beam shot straight up along the line of lockers. The entire mass tipped toward them.

"The hallway!" yelled Frank, gesturing ahead. And both men ran for it.

Frank arrived first and looked back. The long line of heavy metal came crashing down on top of Wilkes and smacked him hard against the cement.

Five years of dust arose, obscuring everything.

Wilkes was dazed but conscious. His soldier instincts pushed him forward, crawling. He could see Frank's blurred hand extended toward him. He caught the hand and slid from under the wreckage, noticing that only a bench had kept him from being crushed.

"Come on, Wilkes, come on!" yelled Frank.

Arm in arm they made it into the hallway, reptilian cries and the thumping of heavy feet close behind them.

Wilkes aimed his flashlight at the double doors leading upstairs to the gym. They ran toward them.

Frank pushed on one door. It wouldn't open. Pull, don't push! He pulled. Wilkes turned and fired a burst into the black behind them. Angry screams and bullets vibrated up and down the hall. Frank dove through the now open door, Wilkes almost on top of him. Wilkes turned and shoved the barrel of his M-16 through two curved steel handles, effectively jamming the doors shut. Something heavy smacked against them; pandemonium on the other side, but the steel held.

They were on a narrow landing. The only light came from a set of windowed doors at the top of the stairs.

"Let's get . . . !" said Wilkes, but he never finished. Instead his head was nearly torn from his shoulders, and his gas can and flashlight clattered to the deck.

Frank spun to see two dim, hulking shapes, one manhandling Wilkes, the other lurching toward him.

Frank was knocked off balance. As he dropped, the gas can

slid from his shoulder. He yanked the .45 from his belt, raised it quickly and fired one round.

The thing cried out, pitched backward.

Quickly, Frank found his feet, retrieved his spray can. His assailant was attacking again. Frank turned and aimed the pistol grip nozzle. He spewed gasoline across its face.

It screamed and fell to the cement, flailing white, caustic smoke.

Frank now could see Wilkes's arm writhing underneath his attacker, slamming a K-bar knife in and out of the fungoid's back. Frank sprayed at close range.

The monster screeched and rolled away from Wilkes.

And Frank stood over it, soaking its smoking head and shoulders until it withdrew into a fetal ball, trying to protect itself.

Frank picked up Wilkes's flashlight and swung the beam toward the other monster, who was trying painfully to crawl up the stairs. The body of the thing was cankered and blotched with recent mold, leaving a trail of browning, smoking slime behind it. The soaked head, dripping gasoline, was different. The light caught the head, which turned, face snarling, eyes aglow.

"My God, Sonny!" cried Frank. "Sonny . . . ?"

Sonny's mouth opened as if to speak. What came out was a spastic distortion—an awful groan. Sonny's eyes blazed furiously for one second, then abruptly glazed over, as if the eyes themselves were dying. Then the boy's head began to droop, his heavy body sagged and a convulsion shook him violently. Within seconds he was unconscious, with his tongue rolling from his mouth.

Frank stood traumatized, then remembered Wilkes.

"Wilkes, you okay?"

Wilkes Bonner gazed at the bloody knife in his hand.

"Yeah . . ."

Frank swung the flashlight beam onto the other casualty.

"That could be Billy . . ."

The face of Wilkes's assailant still was smoking but emerged as Frank stepped closer.

"Good Lord," said Frank weakly.

"That him?" asked Wilkes.

"God, I hope not . . ." replied Frank. He felt a nausea he hadn't experienced since dissecting the belly of his first cadaver.

146

But the corpse was breathing. Air fluttered in and out of the congested airholes centered in its face. A quivering, viscous green lubricant bubbled rapidly from raw glands and sinuses.

"What is it?" asked Wilkes, his voice drained of emotion. "What is that thing?"

Frank forced down the sourness already creeping into his mouth and, licking his dry lips, came closer with the flashlight.

"It's not a 'thing,' Wilkes. This is what a man would look like if I skinned him alive."

"Jesus . . . those eyes . . ."

Air Force dog tags hung around the bloody, muscled neck. Frank bent down, touched the tags with his rubber glove, turning them toward the flashlight. The raised lettering read: "GHISELIN, S.A., SGT."

A guttural moan from behind the locked doors startled them. As Frank turned, he felt extreme pressure on his wrist. When he looked down again, Sergeant Ghiselin's blood-and-muscle hand was locked onto his glove. The lipless mouth stretched wide and a gurgled scream strangled forth, spewing pinkish blood and slime.

Wilkes stood rooted for one tense, unbelieving moment, then leaped forward, and with gloved fist slammed home his knife into the face and neck of the thing. And raging, stabbed it again and again.

Dripping blood like a battlefield surgeon, Frank struggled to his feet; he gripped Wilkes by the shoulders, his own body numb and drifting away from his mind.

"Leave it, Wilkes, leave it . . . for God's sake, man!"

Both men now panted into their masks, both trembling.

Frank managed to kneel beside Wilkes, held him by the back of his head and thrust his own beak forward until both their visors touched.

"Sonny to the hospital, Wilkes! We save Sonny! Help me, okay? Help me!"

Inside his mask, Wilkes's eyes were gorged wide with terror.

"Okay, okay . . ." he mumbled finally.

Frank helped him to his feet.

From behind the doors came a fierce, wailing cry.

Wilkes dropped the bloodied knife from his quivering hand. It clanged noisily to the cement.

CHAPTER EIGHTEEN

Frank pulled the IV dripping dopamine from the vein in Sonny's arm. No blood oozed from the puncture. In fact, as Frank examined the perforation, it seemed to be healing of its own accord. Rapidly, efficiently.

Sonny was stretched nude and unconscious on the operating table. His skin was reddish raw, as if he were relaxing from a steam bath. He breathed slowly and easily. A white bandage covered his left shoulder.

Frank was dressed in standard operating gear: rubber gloves, green lab mask and jacket. Pulling a small penlight from his breast pocket, he leaned over to examine Sonny's eye. He pulled back the lid, punched on the light and was surprised when the pupil refused to shrink.

Frank removed the light as Eric entered the room, carrying a clipboard filled with Sonny's medical charts.

"Mrs. Randolph's in the observation room," said Eric, handing Frank the clipboard.

Frank looked up. Mimi stood at the observation window looking very worried about her grandson.

"We're through here," said Frank to Eric. "You know that bullet wound has practically healed?"

"You're kidding?" said Eric.

"Nope, another fascinating side to 'oddball.' Could be the fungus has properties like penicillin mold, and operating at the speed it does . . ." Frank trailed off.

"Jesus . . ." said Eric quietly.

"Umm . . . can't say it doesn't give its host something in return for the use of its body." Frank glanced quickly at the charts. "Blood pressure's right back to normal; sure as hell wouldn't have thought that. Still plenty of protein serum there. Oh, and speaking of serum, I want you to get the synthesizer ready to travel for tomorrow . . . and a two-month supply of lyophilized enzymes and chemicals."

"The freeze-dried stuff?"

"Yep. May have to last until we can get back to Atlanta."

The synthesizer was their lifeline. It could, bit by bit, put together the DNA sequence for the manufacture of super protein. Once they had a small amount of freeze-dried DNA, they had only to feed it to prepared bacteria. Some of those bacteria then would incorporate the protein into their own DNA, and right away start producing larger quantities, which then would be distilled off the top of the bacterial soup almost like they were making cheap wine. You injected the solution no differently than insulin. Similarly, it coursed throughout the body, penetrating cells, repairing rapidly the damage that was constantly being caused by high levels of radiation. When radiation broke the DNA strands, super protein came to the rescue, traveling rapidly along the DNA strands and rejoining any breaks before they were irrevocably out of place. Though cell engineering still was relatively experimental, the synthesizer never had failed them. With a bit of luck the Vandergot process would continue to save their lives.

Frank punched his digital watch: 5:38 P.M. "Everybody here?"

"Except for Randolph," replied Eric.

"Eric, when we talk to Mimi, don't . . ."

"I won't," said Eric, anticipating Frank's message.

"Try to keep everyone calm."

Eric nodded. Panic would help no one. Frank opened the door to the observation room and motioned Eric through. Mimi continued to stare through the window as they entered.

"He looks awful."

"No, he's okay," said Frank, removing mask and gloves. "The bullet wound's healing nicely. Burns pretty much like

150

Nathan's, slight swelling. In fact, the only thing that's really different is eye movement. I worked a year in the Appalachia region with coal miners. Lighting conditions underground were horrendous, causing gross shifts on the retina of barely visible objects. That's not bad necessarily; you simply begin to see better in the dark and not as well in the daylight."

"You say he's losing his eyesight?"

"No, I'm saying he's okay . . . needs rest, that's why he's sedated." Frank looked around the room. "Did you bring your gear?"

"We're not leaving," said Mimi flatly.

"Mimi . . ."

"This has been my home for over forty years. This is where I'm staying."

"It's not just you. What about Rand . . . ?"

"He won't leave either."

"I can't let you stay *here!*"

Mimi simply picked up her bag from the Naugahide sofa.

"You really do think they'll come tonight, don't you?"

"Yes, I do," said Frank emphatically.

Mimi looked back through the window at Sonny's limp body. "They've captured four of our . . . three of our men and one of our women, who may be sterile. I think they're coming after our women."

Frank hadn't considered this.

"Why do you think that?" he asked calmly.

"No one's consulted me, Frank. But it would seem that a missile command would be womanless. And if they're to survive in their present state, no matter how strange they are, they would have to reproduce more bodies . . . just like we hope to do. Certainly this mutant fungus, fungoid, or whatever you call it, can't do that for them."

Mimi turned and marched toward the hall door. Frank followed.

"Mimi!"

But already she was walking resolutely through the hallway.

"We'll be locked in the church, Frank," she said over her shoulder without breaking stride.

Frank paused in the doorway a moment, helplessly, then turned to Eric.

"I think she's right, you know."

"About the women?" asked Eric.

"Umm . . ." said Frank, pressing his fingers to his temples. The migraine he'd had off and on for two days now, struck another quick, crippling blow.

"Wasn't it Zelda Fitzgerald who said, 'The only thing I *have* to do is die, and I'll never forgive God for that'?"

Upstairs in the hospital recreation room, Anita sat beside Lynne Jenkins, who was taking yet another tranquilizer to calm down. Tears streaked Lynne's mascara as she listened to Velma and Henry sobbing and whispering in the background. Somewhere downstairs they could hear nails being pounded into wood.

Lynne blew her nose into a handkerchief. Her hands fluttered to her lap with an angry sigh as her eyes locked shut.

"Why did these things come here, damnit?"

"I don't know why, Lynne," said Anita quietly. Lynne was a dam about to crack.

Lynne twisted her large, damp handkerchief in her manicured hands, feeling even more wretched, even more outraged as she caressed her husband's embroidered initials. "And what will they do to Roy? My God, this is all so...so...I mean, there are no words for this in the English language. It's beyond comprehension!"

Anita squeezed Lynne's trembling hands and looked pointedly over her shoulder. "Lynne, the children are depending on *us* now. We have to..."

Lynne's red mouth twitched in pain. "If anyone listened to me, we would be leaving here now, right now."

"Shhh..." said Anita, glancing back at the children. "Frank feels it wouldn't be safe tonight, that we're better off waiting till morning."

"Safe?" said Lynne, her voice rising. "What is safe? In five years we haven't known the meaning of the word. For five years we have existed...only...not safe. My God, Anita, between the two of us we have had six miscarriages. That's safe? If we stop taking our miracle drugs, we throw up and defecate ourselves to death. That's not safe. We live under the sword, and the thread of life holding it above our poor heads has never been thinner." Lynne trembled. "And what makes you think we'll make it through till morning? What makes you think we're safe here?" She put her hands to her ears. "God, I wish they'd stop that banging!"

Anita sucked in a deep breath, looked out of the second-story window onto the mall. Dusk. Night was close by. She let out the air slowly, forcing herself to relax, to deal rationally with their dilemma. They would leave tomorrow as planned. They would go down to the sea, to the beautiful sea . . . and begin again.

"Wilkes told me something about those things," said Lynne, lowering her tremulous voice and staring straight ahead. "You won't believe this . . ."

Eric checked the sculptured bars on the ground-floor windows while Frank and Wilkes finished erecting wooden braces inside the hospital doors.

Eric knew the history of the hospital. The bars had been erected during the twenties to keep people in, not out. They were elegantly curled and crafted, but still they were bars. Luckily they had been made strong to last, the way things *used* to last.

Eric tugged hard at each bar, checking the cement foundation at both ends. The windowsills themselves were six feet aboveground. It would be no easy matter just getting to them, much less prying the bars aside.

Eric completed his rounds of the first floor, then went down the hall to help with the barricades. He had a brief argument with Wilkes about erecting a final obstacle in the upstairs hallway.

The result of Wilkes's battlefield mentality an hour later, however, was an eight-foot-high hallway barrier of desks, chairs, tables and file cabinets with loaded rifles and spray tanks nearby at the ready.

For the past few hours they had pushed themselves beyond physical and emotional limits. Now was their most difficult time.

Always the defenders' most onerous task, it was time to wait.

It was almost with relief when, an hour later, they heard the first reptilian roar echo through the mall.

Nathan sat erect, eyes dilated, body shaking violently.

His tongue was huge. He could feel it swelling up inside his mouth, pressuring his jaw, rearranging his teeth, and all about him was the strong smell of disinfectant.

He managed a look around and saw the darkened window, a vase filled with wild flowers on the sill, bare walls of high-gloss white chasing moonlight about an empty room in which he lay bare-chested on a hospital bed.

His entire body ached, worse than a first day of football practice, worse than with the malaria he'd contracted two years ago, worse, much worse. His throat, dry and sore. His eyes painfully out of focus.

He searched his mind for explanations, a point of reference, but found nothing. He was drugged. Yes. That's it. He had felt this way once before. When? After high school? Yes, summer vacation. Working construction in Beaufort. A broken arm. He'd been unconscious. Taken to a hospital. Falling from a roof holding shingles and hammer. His mother standing over him crying as they brought him from the operating room. Internal injuries. Bleeding. Tired. So tired.

Somewhere Nathan could hear human voices calling him. Somewhere distant were voices he knew. Safe voices. He paused to sample his own heartbeat, then drifted off to sleep again.

"I had to talk to you alone, Frank, and I think you know why..." said Anita, closing the laboratory door behind them.

"I do?" answered Frank with a worried smile.

"Yes, you do!" said Anita vehemently. "Look, Frank, I don't need to be so damn overprotected. Just can the perfect southern gentleman bit. I hate getting rumors secondhand!"

"I see," said Frank after a long pause, wondering how much Anita actually did know. He reached out to touch her. She pulled away. He drew up two lab stools. They sat across from each other.

"Did you get this information from Wilkes?" asked Frank, knowing damn well it had to have originated there.

"Wilkes via Lynne. How dare you hold out on me?"

"I'm sorry."

"Well, you should be."

"Not going to be any prettier coming from me."

"Cut the bullshit, Doctor, just tell me."

"Right," said Frank. "Okay, point by point." He paused briefly to choose his words. "Stop me at any point you don't understand."

"Don't be condescending."

Frank stared briefly at Anita. She hadn't changed in the ten years they'd been together; neither had he, of course. Usually their arguments revolved around the same old contentions.

154

"Character flaws," she called them. "Personality differences" was his label. She usually was more direct than he.

"You see, honey," he began, then stood nervously and walked over to the specimen box, "this is a very specialized thing we're dealing with." He tapped the plastic top with a finger. "Half fungi, half algae, it's literally evolved *around* human beings, which means it's specific to humans and only to humans; doesn't affect dogs, cats, rats or anything else. *Capish?*"

"Got it."

"Okay, then, if the body of the human host dies, well, the mutant fungus surviving from it dies too—unless it can find another human host to inhabit."

"Then it is a parasite."

"Well, not exactly. A true parasite destroys, then moves on to its next victim, but, with so few host bodies like ours remaining, this thing can't afford to do that. So instead, it collaborates. And, by developing its thick lichenlike cover, it affords the human body what it so desperately needs—protection from radiation, wounds, and so forth. You following me?"

"Of course."

"Okay, but this is the rough part: To make sure the human body sticks around, this mutant fungoid secretes an acid that eats away the body's skin."

"And that's exactly what I heard," said Anita, trying to deny her queasiness. "So they really are skinless underneath?"

Frank nodded as he sat back down on the stool. "I can't think of a more complete form of domination, can you? Nobody's going anywhere without their skin."

"Why not Sonny? He looks normal."

"Probably the digestive process takes weeks or months," said Frank, lowering his head and staring at the floor. "Then there's another theory, Eric's, though Mimi gave him a starting point."

"What theory?"

Frank looked squarely at Anita. "That this thing, through intimate contact with DNA in the host's cells, is trying to mimic human intelligence, thereby infecting the brain—numbing selective parts of it, like brain cancer."

"You believe that?"

Frank shrugged. "It's already a miracle of adaptation. Eric thinks the next step in its evolution could be to teach its host to appear normal in order to get what it needs. To reproduce new bodies, new hosts—babies."

Anita said nothing for a full two seconds, then pressed against the baby kicking her stomach. "It wants to breed with us?"

"And that would be the ultimate adaptation," said Frank uneasily. "To insure a continuous life cycle."

Frank watched as Anita turned to stare in slack-jawed horror at the specimen box and thought wretchedly, I should have lied.

CHAPTER NINETEEN

Chewing on the stub of a Cuban cigar, Wilkes stared out of the hospital-room window into the mall. Unconsciously, he adjusted the M-16 slung casually over his shoulder.

They were out there, all right, oozing through the shadows, making animal noises at each other. None had come right up to the hospital doors, though. And that bugged him. After all the work he and Frank had put into the barricades, Wilkes wanted them tested. Wilkes liked preparation. For him preparation was everything.

Frank glanced up at the bulldog face stippled with a two-day beard, and he was glad Wilkes was on their side. In Roman days he would have been the faithful centurion. His type hadn't changed much since then, hadn't needed to. There was always a definite need for a Wilkes, especially during emergencies.

A guitar played quietly across the hall.

Anita was singing through a repertoire of songs she had written over the years. Songs to drown out reality, she thought wryly as mutant cries seeped through the two closed windows.

As a teenager growing up in Pacific Palisades, she had begun writing songs for fun, then out of need to explain her own feelings and finally as a means of survival.

There were songs about her mother, the fairly well-known movie actress, and about her famous father, about her first love, about leaving California after high school for good, about backpacking hand-to-mouth across Europe, about waitressing in New York City. About crowded subways. About her first cat. About runaways. About the pond in Central Park. About confusion. About drugs. About drifting. About meeting Dr. Frank Alden, when, one hot summer night, she had ended up with a serious drug problem at Bellevue. About falling in love, really in love, for the first time in her life. About meeting Frank's parents in Richmond, Virginia. About a wedding to which her parents were not invited. About becoming a doctor's wife. About playing the part. About life in the Deep South. About second thoughts, resentments. About working it out, most of it, anyway. About falling in love once again.

There were lots of songs in Anita's repertoire.

"The one about the sailor?" asked Velma excitedly.

"Who leaves home?"

"No, who goes back again, you know, to see his mother."

"Oh, yes, that one," said Anita. "Let's see if I can remember the chords."

Eric lay on one of the hospital beds reading an old *Science Digest* by flashlight. Henry and Lynne played gin rummy by candlelight at the card table. Everyone studiously avoided listening to anything beyond the window.

Anita played the song partway through, then stopped. Velma watched her fingers caress the strings, wishing she knew how to play the guitar. Something very sensual about guitar playing.

"Want to sing along?" asked Anita.

"Sure," said Velma. "I want to learn the words, too."

"Really?" said Anita, smiling. She felt complimented.

"Really," said Velma, laughing for the first time. She liked Anita a lot. They'd always been good friends.

Anita began, and Velma picked up the words a fraction later.

> "When I was very young
> My mother said to me,
> Joe, you're different from your countrymen
> You'll run away to sea.
> Well, Mama's very old today
> Her eyes too dim to see
> So I go back home from time to time
> When it's painful to be free...."

Velma always came in strong on the chorus. For some reason the chorus brought happy tears to her eyes. You could sing out and really taste the words.

"Oh, I must be where the strong winds blow
But I'll see you, Mama, before I go!"

Across the mall in the church, Mimi sat at the organ playing "Onward, Christian Soldiers," drowning monstrous cries with God's spirit.

In a ruptured steam tunnel beneath the university, rats gnawed at something bloody. Then the largest rat looked up from this evening meal, sniffed the air . . . stiffened, and suddenly squeaked out a warning that drove the pack to cover. Seconds later, a multitude of heavy feet came trampling through their appetizer.

"I felt better when I could hear those monkeys," said Wilkes, draining a can of warm Schlitz and lining it up with two other empties on the windowsill. "You think they know we're here?"

"I'd stake my life on it," said Frank. His watch flashed 10:30 P.M. He and Wilkes both were seated in hardback chairs beside the window overlooking the mall.

Wilkes stared into the blackness below and wiped his lips with the back of his thick hand.

"A guy I knew in North Korea," began Wilkes, not checking to see if Frank actually was listening, "he always carried two sidearms—one on each hip; two knives—one on each leg; a sawed-off shotgun and a rifle. Was proficient in jujitsu and had a black belt in karate. Ready for anything, this little guy was. We were dug in near a little town called Waegwan. It was dark about this time, and Kelly was in his hole takin' a crap. In his helmet. That's the way you did it if stuff was going off over your head. Well, no sooner had Kelly sat down on his pot than a North Korean sapper jumped into his foxhole with him. We heard a lot of yellin' and screamin' and it sounded like somebody was gettin' murdered. When we reached Kelly, he was bare-assed and the gook was dead beside him." Wilkes smiled and shook his head. "Kelly had everything but the atom bomb and ended up beatin' a gook to death with his own shit pot."

Frank looked at Wilkes and said nothing. He had no idea what to say.

* * *

Max dozed at Anita's feet as she whispered her last song to Velma and Henry, who both seemed to be fast asleep on the bed.

> "Our minds went a-wanderin' one pure August day
> We sailed like two seabirds through fine ocean spray
> Oh, the colors of rainstorms,
> Oh, the colors of sea
> Be bold with faint colors
> When you're thinkin' of me."

Anita stopped playing and hugged her guitar. Then she stared down at Velma and Henry and smiled. They were so beautiful, these children's faces. So very beautiful.

Gently at first, the heavy padlock on the door to the hospital furnace room began to jiggle. Then, gradually, more force was applied from within. The lock and the door could hold, probably, but not the hasp. Screws already were coming loose from the old wooden doorjamb.

How long has it been since I've eaten? thought Nathan. His eyes opened. He moved an arm first, testing it, then a leg. Everything working. Nothing broken. He sat up on one elbow, took a deep breath, withdrew the white hospital sheet and reached down one pajamaed leg to the cool linoleum.

He slid from the bed onto both knees and suddenly found himself in the position he'd assumed every night as a child, just before his prayers. He gagged as a horrible wine turned disinfectant surged up through his stomach and forced him to his feet.

Yes, I'm hungry, he thought. So hungry.

The door was not locked. He opened it and walked into the quiet hallway.

A few doors down, illuminated by a small kerosene lamp, he could see the jumble of the improvised barricade, and Wilkes braced against the wall, dozing with his face against his rifle.

Another faint light glowed from the room across the hall. Nathan walked softly toward it on bare feet.

In the two darkened rooms on either side of him people were breathing slowly, sleeping.

Anita sat alone in her room playing solitaire, her back to the open door. A single candle flickered from the center of the card table. A pile of sandwiches in wax paper was stacked in a basket near the cards, surrounded by pull-top cans of tomato juice. The window at the far end of the room was shuttered now. The door behind her closed noiselessly.

A dark hand touched Anita's shoulder. Her eyes widened, she sucked in her breath and whipped her head around. Max, sleeping at her feet, awakened, growling. Nathan snatched back his hand, then whispered, "Didn't mean to scare you, Anita."

He tried to pet Max, but the dog snarled, showing his long teeth. "Easy, boy, easy..." said Nathan.

Nathan glanced back at Anita, who still had her slim hand pressed anxiously to her breast.

"Oh...oh...Nathan," she said, still gasping.

"I'm hungry. Is there anything to eat?"

Anita caught her breath. She stood, and drew away from Nathan to get a good, careful look at him. Max remained stock still, awaiting a verdict.

Nathan smiled, and though unsteady on his feet, looked hungrily at the food on the table.

"I didn't want to wake anybody up. What time is it?"

Anita glanced quickly at her watch. "About two-thirty." She paused. "Your fever's gone?"

"I guess," said Nathan, reaching out to pat his dog. Max finally wagged his tail and came over to sniff his master's legs. "I'm still weak but...thank you."

Anita smiled finally. She reached into a basket, retrieved a sandwich in wax paper. She placed it opposite her, then gathered up her playing cards. "Tomato juice?"

"Guess I'm thirsty too," said Nathan.

Anita sat a pull-top can beside the sandwich. "You're not going to eat standing up?"

"No," said Nathan, grasping the back of the chair tentatively.

He sat slowly...gratefully. Anita sat across from him. Max flopped down at her side.

The wobbling hasp on the basement door now was secured by only two screws. With one solid push it popped away from the doorjamb and fell to the linoleum. The door swung open.

Wilkes awakened to the sound. He blinked rapidly, was about to get up and looked around when he heard the murmur of voices and saw light coming from beneath the door to Anita's room. He yawned, glanced at his watch, checked his weapon, then settled against the wall once more, trying to keep his eyes open.

Treelike shapes funneled up the basement stairs and into the first-floor hallway. Amazingly soft-footed, they drifted through the dark toward the stairwell. And though they were creatures born of Stygian clouds, bacteria and primordial mud, their coordination of movement was soldierlike—fantastic yet deadly.

Frank dozed by the window overlooking the mall, his chair cocked against the wall, spray can and rifle on the floor. He opened his eyes, yawned and stretched out his arms from stiff, aching shoulders. The window was open and he was cold without the Windbreaker he had left in the room across the hall.

He rocked his chair to the floor. He stood, rubbed his eyes, picked up the rifle and slung it across his shoulder.

In the hallway Wilkes was snoring, his head balanced against a sofa leg protruding from the jumbled barricade.

Frank decided not to wake up Wilkes, then walked silently across the hall. When he touched the doorknob, he heard Nathan's voice inside. Frank's pulse quickened. He threw open the door.

Anita smiled at her husband. Nathan stood. Frank paused, lost for words.

"Hi, Doc," said Nathan, somewhat timorously extending his hand.

Frank glanced down at the coffee-dark hand for only a second, then clasped it firmly, placing his other arm around Nathan's bare shoulders.

They hugged, then drew back, both very relieved.

"Welcome, Nathan," said Frank with feeling. "Thought we'd lost you yesterday."

"Don't remember much. You'll have to fill me in, I'm afraid." Nathan's fingers brushed hot tears of relief from his eyes. "Damn, it's good to be here," he said with his old familiar grin. "Damn, it's good, Frank."

The army was on the stairs. The moon from the stairwell window lit their way as they gathered forces behind the fire door to the second story. Strict discipline here. Not a sound uttered as the pack leader cracked a fire door and peered down the long, dark corridor into the barricade.

The gnarled face beneath a partial veil of Spanish moss blinked a few times through deep, spongy eyeholes. He turned to give a silent command, then scuttled forward through the door on all fours.

Sonny lay flat on his hospital bed, his face in the moonlight, eyes open. Slowly he turned his face into shadow, thus exposing his left ear.

A dark green spot leaked from his ear canal, spreading out along his jawline.

"I vaguely remember being attacked in a kind of tunnel," said Nathan, sitting again. "Smashing at something I'd already shot...it smelled dead...like a dream...it..."

Nathan shook his head slowly and stared at the candle. His voice faded out as he remembered Billy Van Patten's bloated body floating faceup in the river.

"The only place like that around here," said Frank, "would be the old heat tunnels." He frowned at Anita. "I'll bet that's how they broke into the gym. The damn tunnels run through every building on campus...including this one."

Frank shifted his rifle. "Think maybe I'll check out the basement." He glanced at his watch. "Like Wilkes said, things seem much too quiet."

Wilkes snored heavily, his monotonous wheeze echoing through the barricade and down the long, black hallway. His head, much lower now, leaned into the sofa itself.

On the opposite side, the attack force edged silently to the base of the barricade, invisible but for slight movements in the wavering shadows, when slivers of light from Wilkes's kerosene lamp filtered through the tangle of furniture.

Wilkes's heavy chin was doubled up against his chest, his face in profile. If he could have awakened and turned his head, he would have seen the lichen-covered horror that once was a human face working its way beneath a chair and desk toward him. It wriggled and twisted, contorting its fungoid body, its sunken yellow eyes coming closer, much closer. Then, very slowly, the aberrant reached out its diseased paw to touch Wilkes's face. It stretched and strained, but a heavy file cabinet protected Wilkes by less than an inch.

The thing pushed its leg against a rear support.

Something creaked. Something shifted. Wilkes's small eyes

winked open, darted, blurred, then focused on the sluglike appendage reaching for his nose.

The leader shrieked and thrust forward violently.

Wilkes fell over sideways, screaming himself. In seconds, everything, including Max's frantic barking, was drowned out by a host of ear-splitting yawpings.

Surprise was complete, sending shock waves up and down the dark corridor.

Wilkes, still on his knees screaming, grabbed for his fallen rifle. Frank rushed from Anita's room. Nathan stumbled out behind him.

A large chair from the top of the pile came crashing to the floor. Other pieces of furniture were pushed or pulled out of place. Frank raised his rifle as the first dimorphic shape appeared at the top of the pile. An automatic burst drilled the shadow from its perch.

"WILKES!" cried Frank. "GAS! GET THE GAS!"

First Wilkes blasted away at the barricade, then, acknowledging Frank, staggered to his feet and lumbered toward a brightening doorway.

Lynne turned up a Coleman lantern just as Wilkes entered. Velma and Henry sat up in their beds, terrified.

"Where're the goddamn tanks?" bellowed Wilkes, squinting against deadly whiteness.

Lynne looked behind her frantically, pointed to the spray cans all in a row beneath the window. "There! There! Did they attack?"

"Yes . . . gimme two. I can't see a goddamn thing!"

Lynne handed Wilkes two spray tanks, and he lurched back through the doorway, looping one canvas strap over his shoulder.

Frank, Nathan and Eric were in the hallway now. Eric carried a rifle and a small flashlight. The beam darted across the falling barricade.

A bed smashed to the floor.

A chair fell, snapping its legs.

A hole was gradually opening at the center. Wilkes handed a tank to Frank.

Anita, struggling with another tank, raced from Lynne's room. She gave the tank to Nathan.

Anita then removed Frank's automatic from her dress pocket. She stared at the weapon, wondering if it were ready to fire and if, in fact, she could pull the trigger.

Henry arrived with another M-16. Velma held a flash lantern, its beam picking up glow-eyed tree faces stranger than her wildest fantasy.

Only a desk and file cabinets remained at the center of the barricade. A clutch of glistening fungoids began crawling over it.

"Give 'em the gas! *Now!*" ordered Frank.

Spray tanks spewed forth gasoline like acid, hitting the puffed alien bodies squarely.

Their heads roared in agony and they flopped back across this final obstacle in billows of white smoke, skins browning, sloughing off onto the floor.

Frank yelled back to Anita. "Get ready to lock yourself in a room with the kids!" He was expecting a charge, the suicidal kind, made popular on Guadalcanal, Iwo Jima and Peleliu during World War II. A *banzai* of shrieks, topped by a quivering wall of bloody, smoking flesh.

But . . . the charge did not come. Instead, the metal desk and file cabinet were pulled slowly aside.

Seconds passed. Still no charge.

Silence. Interminable. Frank, Wilkes and Nathan fingered the steel triggers of their spray guns. Eric and Henry held M-16's, flanked the three men. Velma manned the flash lantern. The only other light by the barricade was the dim kerosene lamp Wilkes had used earlier.

Anita stood between Frank and Wilkes, the .45 dangling loosely in one hand, the other hand crossed protectively over her belly. Lynne hovered beside Anita, holding a loaded rifle in each hand.

There was a single awful moan from the blackness beyond the barricade.

Slowly a lone figure shuffled into view, arm locked across its face, groaning. It stopped dead center in the barricade, not crossing the line, growling at the brightness.

"Cut the light, Velma," said Frank.

The lantern went out. Only Wilkes's kerosene lamp on the green linoleum flickered.

The monster dropped its bulbous arm, and standing in the shadows, made a crooning, plaintive sound. Its sickly yellow eyes focused straight ahead as if in a trance. Its paw was cupped between its legs.

Keening its melancholy song, it fixated on Anita and began to fondle itself.

Frank glanced back quickly at his wife. He could not believe the look of revulsion on her face as she raised the .45.

Anita squeezed her eyes shut, and tears ran down her cheeks as her finger froze on the trigger.

For seconds, nothing happened. Then she opened her eyes angrily like any mother defending her child, and the gun went off like a howitzer. It bucked upward, ejecting its spent brass shell.

Her obscene lover catapulted backward into darkness.

And war began with its usual earnest brutality.

As the first rank charged, Velma flicked on the lantern. Simultaneously, bullets and gasoline knocked them flat and screaming onto the green deck. But there were more—they were more than willing to pile up on the wriggling, smoking bodies beneath them. And still more came, decimated, fuming bodies twisting, reaching out bloody, skinless arms. Screaming through lipless mouths. Gaining inches through sheer numbers, like lemmings driven to attain some fearful goal far beyond rational comprehension.

Frank and Wilkes and Nathan sprayed the crawling bodies, but they were coming now in coordinated waves.

"WILKES!" screamed Frank above the din.

"YEAH!"

Frank pointed. "BOLT YOURSELF INTO THAT ROOM! ERIC!"

"WHAT?"

"GET SONNY! LOCK HIM IN TOO!"

"RIGHT!"

Eric emptied his magazine, then raced down the dark corridor into Sonny's room. He yanked at Sonny's narrow bed, which was on caster wheels, and struggled to pull the heavy load through the door.

The whining gunfire and resultant screams were deafening. Frank looked over his shoulder at Eric, then back to Wilkes.

"HELP HIM!"

Wilkes dropped back quickly, grabbed the other end of Sonny's bed and almost heaved it into Lynne's room.

"EVERYBODY ELSE IN OUR ROOM!" cried Frank. "HURRY, DAMNIT. I'M RUNNING OUT OF FUEL HERE!"

The hallway cleared quickly. Henry pulled Max by his collar.

But host bodies staggered forward, swimming in their own gore, nuclear gargoyles programmed to procreate or die, wearing no masks, no faces at all, some missing the entire rind of their bodies and trailing through the white, thinning smoke a stinking brown sludge.

As Velma disappeared inside her door with her lantern, the hallway darkened. Nathan reached for the light, bobbled it.

It smashed to the deck, extinguished.

Frank felt his way backward along the enameled wall.

"Light! Give me some light!" he cried.

A door across the hall slammed shut. The small flashlight Anita handed Nathan fired its beam close by onto an anatomical study with eyes like golf balls hanging from loosely muscled sockets.

Frank was beside the open door now. He tried to struggle through but slid on a gasoline slick.

As the blinded monster lurched forward waving the stump of its arm, Nathan grabbed Frank by the hand. Half crawling himself, Frank was yanked into the room.

Nathan turned and threw his weight against the metal door, slamming it hard. Frank was on his feet. He twisted the key in the sliding steel bolt. It slid home with five separate snapping turns.

Heavy, comforting sounds.

As clawed, skinless fists pummeled the heavy steel.

As yellowed teeth gnawed on the locked handle.

In the room opposite, Lynne struggled to her feet, a wailing Medea. Wilkes lunged against her, trying to hold her arms.

"Where are the kids?" she screamed over the gawping cries from the hall.

"In the other room!" he yelled. "They're in the other room!"

"I want those kids with me, damnit!"

She broke away from him and hurled herself toward the metal door. The key still was in the lock.

Somehow she managed to throw the bolt three turns before Wilkes could pry her hands away.

"They're safe! Safe with Doc!" cried Wilkes.

"NOOOOOOOOOOOOOOOOOOOOOOOOOOO!" she shrieked.

Wilkes slapped her hard across the face. For a second, her eyes cleared. She stared at him, surprised, her lip cracked and bleeding.

"It's gonna be all right!" said Wilkes. "Look, it's gonna be all right! Sorry, Lynne, but you can't go out there!"

He gathered her into his arms as best he could. He patted

her hair with the only tenderness he knew. She whimpered back in short, muscular breaths.

In the far corner of the room Eric was doubled over the sink, his stomach heaving in abject, numbing horror.

No one, however, had paid the slightest attention to Sonny.

Though the shadow side of his face was partially covered with spreading fungus, his expression was one of a sad-eyed Jesus. Yes, he stared with pity at his old friends—those who must be converted—and hid his radiant green baptismal hands beneath the sheet of his bed.

CHAPTER TWENTY

Dawn on campus. The sky was aglow, almost pink outside the hospital window.

Anita had been awake for hours, imagining, staring out of the window at this remarkable sun, in itself a poem, providing inspiration and the courage of life.

The door held securely, as some mad-asylum architect years ago had designed it to do. How much luckier could they be? She thought of Randolph and the decomposing devils that haunted his daily dreams. Was Randolph trying to tell them something? Were he and Mimi safe in the church? Enough.

Enough to watch the sun rise, to cast its light on the slumbering faces surrounding her—the brave army that last night had defended her, the pregnant queen.

Max lifted his sleepy head and yawned; his pink tongue curlicued. He blinked at Anita, then gazed fuzzy-eyed at Henry, who was lying next to him. He couldn't resist those freckles and gave Henry's cheeks and chin two good licks.

Henry's eyes flipped open, startled for only a second.

Anita, who was sitting in a straight-backed chair, grinned. Henry rubbed sleep from his eyes.

"Are we leaving today?" he asked in a voice that though

hoarse from the night before, was more interesting without its usual whine.

Anita nodded. "We're going to live on a sailboat," she whispered. "How's that sound?"

"On the water?" asked Henry. He liked water to drink, to float on, to throw in plastic bags.

"Where else, Henry?"

Velma was awake now, leaning on one elbow, rediscovering her wristwatch. "Has to be a big boat. There's eleven of us."

Anita gazed at Frank, who still was snoring lightly, sitting cross-legged in the corner of the room with his head pressed up against the stock of his rifle.

"Twelve..." said Anita.

Velma frowned, as if demanding a recount. "Twelve?"

Anita patted her stomach. "I had my first contraction an hour ago."

"Oh..." cried Velma spontaneously. "Oh...!" she repeated ecstatically as she rose to hug Anita. Henry looked kind of stunned, as if something more were expected of him.

Frank lifted his head slowly, deep-set shadows beneath his eyes.

"What's wrong?" he asked, coughing instantly but checking heads around the room.

Velma looked first to Anita for permission to break the news. Anita nodded.

"Mrs. Alden is in labor!"

"You're what?" said Frank incredulously, even though the baby was due.

Anita shook her head, her mouth a perfect Mona Lisa smile.

"My God, why didn't you wake me?" said Frank, struggling to his feet.

"I wanted you rested for delivery, Doctor," she said, reaching out to him.

"Honey..." he said, holding her back to look into her eyes. "We'll have to move fast now."

"Don't worry," she said, "this babe is not coming out till I'm damn good and ready."

Frank laughed. "That's telling him!" He glanced at the door, then, more soberly, to Nathan, still fast asleep on a bare mattress. "How's he doing?"

"Looks all right to me," said Anita, moving to Nathan's side. She shook him gently as Frank stepped carefully around

170

beds and bodies and tiptoed to the door. He put his ear to the cool metal.

"Nathan . . . Nathan . . ." said Anita, gently.

"Shhh . . ." said Frank, thinking he'd heard something in the hallway.

"Wilkes! Wilkes!" Frank called through the door. There was a long pause.

"Morning . . ." whispered Nathan, eyes still closed.

"Good morning, Nathan," said Anita. But she too was looking at the door now.

"Wilkes!" yelled Frank again.

Still no answer, only the cawing of crows settling into the vegetable garden outside the window, as if they knew the people were leaving.

"Damnit . . ." muttered Frank. He looked anxiously at Nathan. "We don't need any more surprises."

The hot Georgia sun was just above the distant trees, splashing the hospital room with sudden intense brightness. Nathan squinted, rubbed his eyes, sat up. He watched as Frank shouldered a spray can.

"Nathan, if you can knock 'em down, I'll spray 'em. Can you back me up?"

Nathan nodded, picked up his M-16, checked the load; he stood, a little wobbly at first. Anita caught him. Nathan straightened.

"No, I'm okay . . ."

Frank took a set of keys from his Windbreaker pocket, placed one in the bolt lock and turned it five times clockwise. He removed the keys, stuck them in his pocket. He placed his ear once more to the metal, then drew away finally, shaking his head.

Henry grabbed Max by the collar.

Frank was tense. "Since those things can't tolerate much sunlight, we *should* be alone now. But just in case, everyone except Nathan move to the window. Give us some leeway."

When everyone was set, Frank unlocked the handle itself, and slowly pressing down, cracked open the door. He could see along the hallway, not quite to the barricade.

Sun filtered through the first few open doors to reveal toppled spray cans, a broken rifle, massive bloodstains across the green linoleum, odd sections of furniture that once had been part of the barricade smashed in frustration against the bullet-pocked walls and floor.

171

Frank stuck out his head farther. Indeed, most all the barricade had been ripped to pieces during last night's frenzy, but . . . there seemed to be no bodies, no casualties left on the battlefield to die.

Frank opened the door all the way. He saw the door to Lynne and Wilkes's room. The door shouldn't have been open, but it was . . . partially.

"Wilkes," cried Frank hopefully, but his heart already was sinking. "Wilkes, are you in there? Eric . . . Lynne?" Again, only the faintly derisive echo of Frank's own voice answered.

Debris stretched before him like a city dump.

Frank motioned Nathan forward, then sprayed the bloody linoleum before them. Nathan followed in Frank's damp tracks.

They crossed the hall. They stood in front of Wilkes's and Lynne's sanctuary. Frank glanced back at Nathan, who raised his M-16, ready to fire. Frank's knuckles were white on the stainless-steel trigger grip of his spray gun.

Frank pushed the door with his boot. It creaked ajar as if slightly bent from its hinges.

When they looked inside, there were no people. There were no signs of a struggle. They stood quietly, aware of their own breathing.

"Could be they're outside?" said Nathan finally.

Frank looked down at Wilkes's spray can and rifle stacked beside the door. "He'd never have gone without these, not Wilkes."

"How'd *they* get through?" asked Nathan, with the accent on dread.

Turning, Frank looked at the steel door itself, grabbed it with his hands and shook it, kneeled before its locking mechanism. The long bolt was thrown wide open.

"There's nothing wrong with this door," said Frank, standing.

"What does that mean?"

"I don't know."

Frank paused, looking very tired, his face puffed and white against two days' growth of graying whiskers. "But we're leaving now."

He looked over his shoulder. Anita stood full and ripe in the doorway across the hall, questioning him.

Frank's jawline went grim. He dropped his eyes, then slowly shook his head. It would be hard explaining to the children.

* * *

Minutes later, everyone filed through the front door of the hospital and onto the sunny mall with its green grass, its vegetable garden and the unperturbable General Lee. Hungry crows flew only as far as the nearest large oak tree.

Seemingly nothing outside had changed. Fanning out, the now shrinking family crossed the mall toward the church.

Frank motioned everyone back as they came close: The empty wheelchair stood on the pavement in front of the church. The heavy front doors to the building were swung wide.

Frank spun the wheelchair around, examining it, then stared into the church. The nave looked serene. Prisms of light from the stained-glass windows threw patches of color on pews and pulpit.

"Mimi!" Frank cried.

There was no answer.

Frank and Nathan entered first, checking every dark corner in the back of the church. A bust of St. Peter studied them intently. An overly sentimental painting of Christ and Mary Magdalen appeared lewd, almost repellent. A marble basin smelled of gassy swamp water. Everyone moved down the aisle ten paces behind Frank and Nathan. Henry carried his M-16 at the ready, his pinched expression that of a young Third World warrior. Velma bore a heavy spray tank across her slender back, her tearful eyes darting from side to side. Anita, in pain, still supported the Army .45. Max limped along in the rear, his cast thumping lightly on the wooden floorboards.

The refugees paused beside the pulpit, stared briefly at the altar with its burned candles and gilt cross.

Without warning the church bell rang. The floor quivered with resonance.

Frank motioned toward the closed rectory door. Max whined. Henry reached for his collar.

Nathan stood beside the door. Frank tested the handle. It was unlocked. Frank signaled to Nathan and in one swift motion threw the door open, letting Nathan thrust the barrel of his M-16 inside.

Inside, Mimi was pouring a huge potful of tea into eleven cups set around the large oak table. She was in profile to the door. From the corner of her eye she saw the door swing open, and as she turned in fright, she almost dropped the pot.

"Oh!" she exclaimed, looking over her bifocals, the door still out of focus.

173

Nathan quickly lowered his rifle. Frank stepped forward apologetically. "Sorry, Mimi, didn't mean to frighten you."

But Mimi kept her hand to her thumping heart. "Did you call when you came in?" she gasped.

"Yes, we did," said Frank, and taking her gently by the arm, he motioned her toward the closest straight-backed chair.

Mimi's breath returned. She smiled wanly. "You see, I had my hearing aid turned down from last night."

She sat and turned up her hearing aid.

"Noisy, weren't they?" said Frank, sitting beside her, noticing tears in Velma's eyes.

"Yes . . . there . . . that's better . . ." said Mimi.

The church bell finished ringing slowly. A door opened. Randolph entered, leaning heavily on his cane.

"The bell was for you . . ." he explained in a flat voice.

"To come to breakfast . . ." said Mimi, quickly adjusting her glasses and clearing her throat. She looked briefly at the battleworn faces surrounding her, then back to Frank. "You have people missing."

"Four," nodded Frank. "Wilkes, Lynne, Eric and Sonny. They were locked in the room across the hall. This morning they were gone."

Velma sobbed once, caught it and held the rest in.

Mimi glanced at Randolph, whose hand was pressed against his twitching face. She continued to pour tea.

"Randolph dreamt there would be . . . fewer of us. Didn't you, Randolph?"

"Yes, Mama."

Mimi finished pouring the tea.

"There . . . everyone please sit."

Frank watched as Anita controlled another contraction.

"We can't stay, Mimi. You see . . ."

"Frank," said Anita, interrupting quietly, "we'll need to eat before we leave. I'm sure Mimi and Randolph will have some packing to do, so . : ."

"Randolph and I are not going with you, Anita," said Mimi matter-of-factly.

She raised her hand before Anita could protest.

"Now, let's everyone sit and join hands around the table." And everyone sat. For a simple but enduring moment, they all clasped hands. All heads bowed except Mimi's. She raised hers, eyes closed, toward the stained-glass windows.

"Beautiful is the sight of many children at play; beautiful

174

the croon of a mother over her babe; beautiful the hand of the newborn. Beautiful is suffering when it flowers into purity of a soul transfigured. Beautiful are the dreams that visit lovers of mankind. Beautiful is heroism that does not see itself. Beautiful is the humility of a strong man." She paused. "Oh, ye memories of love! Bless ye our minds and lift us up forever!"

Daylight shined brightly through the two stained-glass windows. Even when the prayer was finished, no one dropped their hands. No one looked up.

Tomorrow the circle would be that much smaller.

CHAPTER TWENTY-ONE

But this morning was a good time to look at reality. To examine it like a bleached skull. To make difficult but rational decisions.

It was time to say good-bye to a place where they had been encouraged to develop a sense of mutual trust and mutual support in building their small community.

And somehow, on this simple level, they must have succeeded, for they alone had survived a world of mutually assured self-destruction.

Alone.

A fearful word. To be utterly *alone* in a hostile world.

Maybe there *were* other pockets of human existence, but four years had passed since they had heard anything but static on their radio.

Frank drove the little Toyota up Route 95, north toward Savannah, slowing occasionally for abandoned vehicles.

There could be others, he thought. And if they're here, we'll find them.

Frank, Anita and Nathan sat in the front seat. Velma and Henry were in back. The camper top had been removed to accommodate their most needed possessions: the lyophilized chemicals and enzymes recovered four years earlier from the

Center for Disease Control in Atlanta; the synthesizer, which was about the size of an IBM typewriter, full of interlocking plastic tubes and containers, and run by small electric motor; two small Honda generators; spare parts; gasoline; antibiotics; tablets for malaria; a surgical kit; a set of biological-warfare suits with spare oxygen packs; and military cans of insect repellent.

Besides food, they had brought along two goats, six chickens, two roosters, a dozen white mice, Henry's pet rabbit that was pregnant and as much animal feed as possible.

Velma lay on three duffel bags stuffed with clothing and stared up at the clouds. Henry stroked Muriel, the rabbit named after his mother. Max crouched on a soft tarpaulin that covered most of the other gear and coolly ignored the baaing goat tied next to him. Max's colorful plaster cast had been decorated by Henry, always in need of keeping his quick hands busy.

As they neared Savannah, they passed a gutted school bus with its blistered yellow paint, a child's red lunch box that lay open on the road and contained a plaid thermos and a squared aluminum foil that once protected a tuna fish sandwich.

They arrived at a cliff where the highway ended in a deep volcanolike crater partially filled with water.

They detoured across fields and through streams, sometimes getting out to push the little overloaded truck.

They discovered the white bones of dead farm animals, toured forests of charcoal-black trees, skirted small ghost towns with falling-brick buildings, cracked barber poles, looted drugstores, supermarkets trailing boxed and bottled wares through broken windows, where the contents had then been picked over by those with stomach complaints and migraine headaches, people in need of a gentle, soothing laxative, a tranquilizer or rat poison.

And all the while, Anita's labor pains were coming closer together.

Having moved across the border into South Carolina, it was late afternoon before they arrived at their destination, a port that Henry's grandfather, an ex-Union Bag president and ham radio buff, had told them five years ago was still intact, for it had been spared the holocaust of fires that raged up and down the East Coast.

They drove past a main gate, past the quarter-million-dollar homes where moneyed southern gentry and their carpetbagging northern equivalents had once retired to a life of golf, tennis and sailing.

Past a faded wooden sign that said "Port Royal."

Then, in the amber sunlight, a lighthouse, fashioned more for charm than function, appeared over treetops before them.

And the Toyota rolled slowly through a small and attractive pedestrian shopping mall.

It passed an art gallery with typical marine paintings in rich golden frames; a clothing store still displaying exquisite 1983 fashions worn by straight-nosed mannequins, their elegant faces partially obscured by intricate spider webs, their dresses unmarred by price tags.

They passed an intimate portside restaurant advertising Bert Lamar at the piano bar; outside racks stuffed with rusting bicycles; and, of course, the inevitable knickknack shop with cute but expensive toys for adults.

The Toyota left the mall and moved onto the cement walkway surrounding the man-made harbor.

Boats of every size and shape flashed their thoroughbred credentials of epoxy paint and stainless steel. A few had sunk, but most still were tied to the cement with nylon lines, waiting patiently to be taken to sea.

The truck stopped. Everyone got out, pointing to this boat and that. There was great excitement about finding the right home.

Frank talked to Nathan as they walked beside a giant Chris Craft. Anita brought up the rear with the kids and Max. She obviously was hurting, but the joy of actually being here, of being alive and well, was more than compensation. Harbors and boats pointed the way toward a new kind of life—a new world.

Anita felt tears in her eyes, and thought improbably, This time if we discover Indians, they can teach us a few things.

This time.

Frank and Nathan rounded the bow of a giant cruise boat, and a forty-five-foot motor sailer appeared. They stopped dead in their tracks, stared at the name *Edith's Joy* painted astern.

"This might be it," said Nathan. "Let's take a look."

They walked forward, lightly, like two teenagers planning a raft voyage down the Mississippi.

"Not new, but damn good design," said Nathan with a wide sweep of his hand. "Fiber glass hull with teak deck, mahogany trimming, just a little linseed oil and..." He smiled at the automatic wind tiller and then up at the two strong wooden masts. "My God, Frank, it's perfect!"

As Nathan clapped Frank on the back and hopped aboard, a mother sea gull screamed up from her nest on the forward deck. Max broke away from Henry to bark at the bird circling nervously in the mauve-colored sky.

Frank extended his hand and helped Anita on board. Together now, the family walked up to the forward deck to stare with appreciation at a nest cleverly fashioned in a coil of anchor line. The nest contained three brown-speckled eggs. A small white dinghy protected its western perimeter.

"You think she would mind if we moved her home over to the Chris Craft?" Nathan asked Anita.

"As long as we're careful with her eggs," answered Anita with a pale smile.

She was very tired now, the contractions coming with more intensity, about ten minutes apart. The ocean air helped. It blew stronger as the tide changed. It danced in across the cay, whipping the marshes and chopping up the green water beyond the port. And suddenly she was back aboard another sailboat at Marina Del Rey near Los Angeles, where her dad had lived just after divorcing her mother. Where he lived and wrote his melancholy poetry that some people seemed to like, for they bought it in great quantities when he published each year. Never great poetry, but in his crude way he'd touched a wide range of unhappy teenagers who understood what he was saying because their hearts and sensibilities were wounded in the same immature way as his. And when the two of them were together aboard the boat, not even at sea but tied to the floating docks, she felt the only real closeness she ever would feel toward her father.

So I go back home from time to time
When it's painful to be free.

Writing her own poetry always was difficult, particularly in the shadow of obvious success. So instead she had written what she called "her songs," her personal songs to be sung on special occasions, never to be sold and to be tossed away lovingly like old worn, patched Levi's as she outgrew them.

Oh, I must be where the strong winds blow . . .

She marveled at the swelling deck, gently alive beneath her feet.

But I'll see you, Daddy, before I go.

Yes, they were now going to reexplore the world, to sail oceans if they wanted, to chart strange islands, to live like Ulysses himself. And maybe . . . just maybe to discover others . . . just like themselves.

But best of all—and for some reason the thought brought more tears to her eyes—yes, the very best of all, her baby, her explorer-child, would be born at sea!

A small white wicker table had been placed on the porch of the old colonial Vandergot home. Two crystal glasses sat on the wisteria blue tablecloth. A cut-glass bottle of nut-sweet Duff Gordon sherry reflected the dying sun like a rare amethyst.

Beside the glasses were two small red and white capsules.

Upstairs, Mimi stood in front of the ancient chiffonier mirror that never had reflected a totally accurate image. The wallpaper of decorative magnolia blossoms reflected behind her had browned appropriately over the years and the room seemed to smell of their darkening fragrance.

She was keenly aware of the large four-poster, in which she and her husband had shared mutual love and respect for so many years.

Not that they hadn't had their spats too. They certainly had!

Mimi turned slowly, admiring the dress Ben had bought her on their honeymoon in Paris fifty-three years ago. The dress still fit, as did all her other dresses. Except during her one pregnancy she had not gained nor lost more than ten pounds since she'd made her debut at the cotillion in the old De Soto Hotel in downtown Savannah.

Unlike most of her girl friends, she had been presented to society with a group of much younger girls, *after* graduating from college. After college, and not singly, for hers was not a wealthy family. Her family was moderately well off. Her father had taken his Hippocratic oath quite seriously and charged no more than he thought each person, black or white, could afford.

And, my land, the dance had been spectacular! She had

been whirled and turned, and occasionally had taken as many as ten steps before being cut in on by yet another handsome man in white tie and tails.

Till five in the morning they had danced, stopping only briefly to smoke their Pall Malls or Lucky Strikes. And the only whiskey consumed, naturally, was made from corn and hidden away in a silver flask beneath a set of tails, for this was Prohibition.

Perhaps because she was the oldest female at this cotillion, she immediately was attracted to the oldest male—a medical student from Harvard, a Boston Yankee named Ben Vandergot.

They had finished the last dance together and he had driven her home to her house on Oglethorpe Avenue in his red-and-black Hupmobile roadster. And though it was love at first sight, and they talked as lovers do, they hadn't even kissed good night.

Six months later, however, they were thoroughly enjoying their honeymoon in Paris, dancing and drinking champagne and...

Mimi found that she actually was waltzing about the bedroom, holding out her hands as though her slim-figured husband were still as young as he had been then. Still the handsome, charming and sensitive man she had married, who, like her father, had sworn to help free the world of plague and pestilence.

Mimi stood by the doorway and faced into the room. The magnolia blossoms had darkened considerably. It was time.

"Randolph," she called downstairs, "are you ready?"

"Yes, Mama," he answered. "I'm waiting for you in the living room."

Mimi wished the bedroom well, turned and fled down the stairs before she could change her mind, for she knew she was not very brave.

When she passed the mirror at the foot of the stairs, she saw and yet could not see an old lady with a wrinkled face wearing her powder-white hair pulled tightly back in a pony tail. And she smiled.

Randolph stood of his own accord as she floated gracefully into the living room. He raised himself onto one crutch and took her withered hand in his, as if asking her to dance.

Together they walked out the front door, left it open and sat together at the small wicker table. Randolph managed to pull out her chair for her and seat her properly, and she was amazed, for she knew, physically, he hadn't been able to do this since the war.

The gentleman poured, his face becoming beautiful as he did so, no longer scarred, but rather like...yes, rather like Ben's.

The dark sherry filled her glass, then his. And she could smell its pungence.

No words were spoken, but there was no need. They looked lovingly into each other's eyes.

They placed a mutual promise on their tongues and drained the amber liquid from their crystal glasses.

Then standing, they walked hand in hand down the porch stairs, across the darkening mall toward the white church.

And Randolph, who actually had not put the suicide pill in his mouth, let it fall behind them in the damp grass.

CHAPTER TWENTY-TWO

A light breeze blew along the Carolina coast, and the ship's portholes glowed with faint gaslight. *Edith's Joy* now was a black silhouette under full sail, the harbor lighthouse far behind, the only sound heard above deck a hungry goat baaing for his dinner.

Belowdeck on a small galley stove a pot containing scissors, a clamp and shoelaces boiled.

In tears, Henry slammed a large kitchen knife into a cutting board to finish slicing a mammoth red onion.

Velma had forgotten to bring her favorite can opener. She wrestled with the dull, rusted one they'd found on board, cranking away furiously at a big can of Gebhart's chili and beans.

Max, of course, lay as close to their feet as possible, raising his eyebrows hopefully, forcing himself not to whine, not to beg like a dog with less dignity.

Frank stripped a surgical glove from his fingers and placed it into a small trash bag beside the main stateroom bunk.

"Still only seven centimeters; three more to go."

"How much longer?" asked Anita wearily. She was propped up against two orange life vests and a pillow.

"Depends on the dilation," answered Frank, glancing toward

185

the galley. "Too soon to start pushing." He wiped her forehead with a damp cloth. "You're doing fine."

"Doing fine..." she repeated with a groan.

A new contraction grabbed her hard. She reached for Frank's hand, squeezed it for a full thirty seconds before relaxing.

"Five minutes apart now, you're getting there," said Frank. "You're getting there."

Nathan stood at the wheeled tiller and looked up into the black sky, past the huge moon and into the stars. The blazing stars that reminded him of the fireflies on Daufuskie. Or "Fuskie," as they used to call the island, with its oxcarts, old bungalows with faded green shutters, its wood stoves and iron bedsteads, its spartina marshes and bearded oaks, its breakfasts of fried mullet and pullet eggs, its dinners of bluecraw crab, boiled shrimp, biscuits stuffed with ham and sausage... berries... rice.

"Damn, I'm hungry," said Nathan, for the sea air not only reminded him of home, but also charged his appetite.

Funny how meals bring back memories faster than almost anything, he thought. Funny.

If the tide was right, after breakfast on Sundays he and his daddy would take their bateau up a small tidal creek, cut the engine and pole over the finest oyster beds in the South. They'd pitch the oysters into the boat and fill their burlap sacks. Then they'd move on past the beds, roll up their sleeves and grab down deep into silt bottoms until they pulled up black clams by the dozens.

But the casting net or catch net was Nathan's favorite. How old was he when his daddy taught him how to cast? Four or five?

He remembered standing up in the prow with the cotton draw line noosed over his wrist, the "bullet" of one of the net's lead weights in his teeth. His father would pole the boat up to a tidal pool where you could see the water pop as fish tore up their quota of little marsh shrimp.

With a sweep of his arm and putting his entire body into it for a smooth follow-through, he would fling the net spiraling across the water and try to drop all its weights evenly so that on the draw, the mullet, catfish or whatever was underneath would be entangled hopelessly.

And later Sunday night their family and friends would have a feast, a veritable feast!

The gentle swells lifted Nathan's hungry stomach, and to

his surprise, they dropped it again uneasily. An old sour wine was rising. He had been seasick only once in his life, during a freak storm that hit the old mailboat that ran from Savannah to Daufuskie and back three times a week. Why was he thinking of the mailboat? Oh, yes: The only person in the boat who didn't get sick that day was his mother, and only because she was midwifing Emmy Lou Homely, on their way to the hospital in Savannah.

He was ten years old. Emmy's baby boy had been born in the boat right in front of him. And as he had helped his mother stop the bleeding, the placenta had fallen out right on his bare feet.

The boat rolled slowly, and now Nathan glared up at the moon and stars. His face rapidly was becoming a mass of perspiration. His stomach churned mightily from the gentlest of swells.

Henry appeared in the hatchway and stared up the stairs at Nathan.

"Supper's ready, Nathan. Gee, you sure look seasick."

Nathan nodded, forcing his stomach by sheer willpower to behave. "Yeah...well, thanks, Henry...always count on you..."

"Chili and beans," said Henry and disappeared back down the ladder into the cabin.

Nathan wiped his face on the sleeve of his khaki shirt, tried to breathe deeply to control his growing nausea.

He tied fast the automatic tiller. He let himself down through the hatchway.

The hinged mahogany table had been set up. Bowls of chili at each of the three places. Glasses of grapefruit juice.

Nathan tried to smile at Velma as he sat opposite her, but his lips curved down into a painful grimace.

Henry arrived from the galley and put his bowl of onions at the center of the table. Beneath the table, Max whined just slightly.

Nathan glanced away from the chili. Until he heard Anita moaning, he had thought he could pull through this. He could see Frank sitting on the edge of the bunk in the main cabin passing Anita a glass of grapefruit juice. He watched in silent fascination as she drank greedily.

He put the first spoonful of chili into his mouth and was very sorry he'd done so. He stood up from the table, almost knocking it over.

"Nathan . . . ?"

But Nathan slapped his hand to his mouth, apologized to Velma by nodding his head once, then hightailing it, passed Frank and Anita, almost running into the forward gangway. He wrenched open the head door by its brass handle and slammed it behind him. There was an immediate sound of retching.

Velma looked down the length of the boat and turned very pale.

"Think I'll just have juice," she said to Henry.

Henry could see Velma's distress, and despite some recent signs of maturity, reverted to type. He piled in a huge spoonful of chili, letting it drip out slowly from the corners of his mouth. Then he smiled at Velma.

Velma's face went white as lye. She picked up her juice. She tossed it into Henry's grinning face.

The grapefruit juice stung Henry's eyes. He pulled out a red handkerchief from his pocket and tried to wipe away the sting. He could not believe she had done this to him. After all, he was just teasing. He didn't really want to make her sick.

And as he started crying, he suddenly realized that there was no one to take up for him now. Lynne was gone and everybody else was busy.

He blinked back his tears.

He had never seen Velma look so strange, not even when she had punched him in the gym. She was quivering all over.

"No more, Henry."

Velma whispered, so that she wouldn't disturb Frank and Anita. "No more," she said. "Henry, you and I have both lost our parents now and I don't have to feel sorry for you anymore, Henry. I can feel sorry for myself now . . . me . . . I hurt too . . . just as bad as you hurt . . . Henry Baldwin, maybe even worse."

Henry felt awful. He wanted to cry, or to laugh, he wasn't sure which. Instead, he gave his mouth a good, thorough wipe with his red handkerchief.

"Velma," he said finally in a jerky whisper, and felt as though he were drowning in some totally baffling new emotion. "Velma . . . I like you . . . I do . . ."

CHAPTER TWENTY-THREE

They were late for church.

And for the hundredth time Randolph remembered exactly the way it had happened. He had opened the driver door to the new dark blue Chrysler parked in the driveway of their Chevy Chase home; he had turned his head back toward the house just as Gail was hustling Kathy and Cheryl out the front door. Everyone wearing new Easter outfits, all pastels.

He had taken the car keys, the ones on the orange plastic ring, from his dark gray Brooks Brothers suit pocket, unlocked the car door, opened it and hung up his suit jacket on the small metal hook inside.

He had told his family to hurry. He hated being late for church. He remembered the air sucked from his mouth, and billions of well-aimed flashbulbs that turned everyone's skin, muscle and fat translucent. Yes, for that second they had resembled skeletons, like shoes under a fluoroscope. He remembered the old bricks around the doorway caving slowly inward, grabbing the heavy wood doorframe and hurling everything into the foyer.

Randolph remembered getting up from the lawn where he had landed, rushing over to the house, picking up brick after brick until he had uncovered his two daughters and his wife, all still breathing.

He remembered crying for help and finding no one.

He remembered putting his wife and daughters into the car and driving to the Bethesda Naval Hospital.

He remembered leaving his wife and daughters and taking a helicopter to the presidential bunker in the Blue Ridge Mountains in nearby Virginia.

He remembered his own suffering, helping others much worse off than he, and weeks later, the constant smell of death.

He did not remember leaving Washington.

A fat, yellow moon ducked into a spray of filigreed clouds. Bleating sheep huddled nervously on the grassy hillside, as close as possible to the little white church whose doors were thrust wide open.

A scratchy Beethoven sonata played inside.

Outside, a huge alligator plodded up the hill, very sure of a good meal.

Randolph fondled the orange key ring he always carried in his trouser pocket. It reminded him of a badly fried egg. He took out a book of matches. He lit the candles in candelabra on either side of his mother, who lay in state on the church altar.

He paused, then leaned forward and touched her stone-cold lips with his.

He listened a moment to Beethoven on the old Victrola he'd placed in the aisle, and when finally he stepped backward, he staggered, for he was without crutches.

Slowly he dropped to his knees and prayed.

To whom?

Whom could he trust? God? No. He was alone.

He cried.

Like a finger down a chalkboard, the steel needle scraped across the old RCA record. And the music died.

A pause.

Randolph heard soft, padding footsteps behind him.

Painfully he arose, forcing his legs to accept his fragile body one last time.

"Hello, Sonny," said Randolph, staring into his son's sad eyes. Randolph gestured to the half-human monstrosities arranged in front of the first pews. He could barely recognize Wilkes, Lynne and Eric in the front rank.

"You're not lookin' too bad," Randolph said with a smile. "I mean, compared with the others."

Sonny did not move, blink or even look human. He just stood there looking so sad, like those fake Christs who stare out of fake paintings with their crying eyes rolled to heaven and their quaking mouths. Yes, Sonny was a good copy, but there was no life in those eyes, thought Randolph. Just despair.

Sonny was totally nude, as if to advertise the fact that he carried no weapons, as if to infer that he was harmless. He stepped forward and reached out a spotless hand to touch Randolph's cheek.

Randolph stepped back and drew from his belt the chrome-plated .38 that once had been his father's.

Sonny lowered his hand, his expression even more pained.

"I used to love my son," said Randolph, the pistol still aimed at Sonny's face.

Randolph got a good grip on himself. He pulled back the hammer of the pistol. "I'm not going with you—to hell," he said forthrightly.

Sonny opened his mouth slightly. Through green, bubbling slime, he croaked something that vaguely sounded like "Father" and stepped forward to kiss his father's cheek, as southern sons normally will do.

Randolph smiled and brought the barrel of the .38 to his own white-haired temple. He pulled the trigger.

Eyes clenched. Blood gushed. He toppled into the simple blackness he so earnestly desired.

Sonny gazed down sadly at his father's head haloed in blood on the church floor.

CHAPTER TWENTY-FOUR

Frank leaned forward holding both of Anita's hands, talking to his wife, consoling her, encouraging her as if the birthing required two people instead of one.

"How long does it take to have a baby?" asked Henry, still eating.

"Depends," said Velma. "My mother told me I took forty-eight hours."

"Like that?"

Henry gestured into the main cabin. "Does she have to breathe like that?"

"It's called the Lamaze method. It's supposed to be less painful."

"Boy, I sure wouldn't want to have a baby," said Henry earnestly as he put away another lump of canned pear.

"Don't suppose you ever will," said Velma, grinning. Henry had been okay since their showdown.

"Guess not," said Henry.

Henry stood and gulped down his third glass of grapefruit juice. "Well, I have to go to the bathroom."

Velma was alarmed. "You feel sick too, Henry?"

"Just a pee." Henry shrugged, giggled self-consciously and sauntered awkwardly away from the table.

Velma watched him go. Henry just now was beginning to enter the real world of human feelings. Already she felt closer to the boy.

Henry stopped in front of the head. He knocked gently on the closed door.

"Nathan . . . ?"

There was no answer. Henry reached for a tiny kerosene lamp hanging on the wall of the passageway behind him. He turned the brass door handle, half expecting it to be locked. The handle dropped and Henry opened the door, pushing the light in first ahead of him.

The bathroom was empty.

Good, thought Henry. Nathan's probably lying down in the front cabin. He sure looked awful.

Henry hung the little lamp from a towel rack, everything within his reach. He was beginning to like boats. They were designed for people his size. Most houses made him feel too small.

Henry lifted the toilet-seat top.

Deciding he had to do more than pee, he unbuckled his belt, unzipped his corduroy trousers and was about to pull down his Fruit of the Loom underpants when he glimpsed something in the toilet bowl.

Something.

"Damn," said Henry. "At least Nathan could flush . . ."

He stared down between his legs.

He froze.

Whatever it was in the toilet was moving a little.

Spreading.

"Oh, shit!" cried Henry, leaping away from the toilet. He yanked up his skivvies and trousers with one swift jerk and smacked his head against the door behind him.

"Damn!" he cursed, trying to stand on the heels of his bare feet.

Gotta get outta here . . .

Henry grabbed the door handle, yanked it down and swung into the mahogany-paneled corridor.

"Doc!"

Busy with Anita, Frank did not turn immediately. Velma, however, saw Henry standing down the dim corridor buckling

194

his belt. She saw the forward cabin door open. Saw Nathan appear in the shadows behind Henry, looming over the child.

"HENRY!"

Max scrambled up from under Velma's feet, barking like crazy, and took off toward the other end of the boat.

Henry and Max passed each other in midcabin, and Frank reached out his hand to stop Henry.

"Henry . . . ?" he called, but Henry ran like a rabbit, scampered up the ladder through the main hatch onto the deck.

Frank spun to his feet at the urgency of Max's barking.

"Max! Max! Come here!"

"What's wrong, Frank?" asked Anita in midcontraction.

"Don't know . . . Max is down by the head going after Nathan." Painfully Anita grasped both wooden sides of the bunk and pushed herself up from the kapok pillows. "I think we'd better get up on deck."

"Are you serious? We can't . . ."

Nathan kicked Max. The dog yelped once, rolled backward, scrambled to his feet and attacked once more. The dark giant advanced into the light.

"Oh, my God!" exclaimed Frank. "He's . . ."

Anita already was on her feet, leaning against Frank for support. "On deck . . . on deck . . . !"

Velma stood up from the table, rigid.

Frank and Anita struggled toward her. Max slashed and snarled. A wailing cry filled the boat, and Velma fled through the galley into the cabin behind her. She ducked inside the door, closed it, locked it securely and shook from head to toe. She could hear Henry yelling from the deck to Frank and Anita.

"Hurry! *Hurry!*"

Henry reached out his hand and clasped Anita's. Frank pushed. Henry pulled.

Anita could taste her own tears as Henry guided her up the ladder.

"I'll take care of you! I'll take care of you!" cried Henry. He tried to catch Anita before she fell onto the teak deck, but they rolled on top of each other.

"My baby! My baby!" cried Anita.

Velma stood with her back to the door, still quivering. Frank called her.

She sucked in her breath but didn't move.

"VELMA! Where are you?"

Frank started toward her cabin. Nathan tried to follow, his

eyes glazed yellow, his face sweaty, distorted, the horror inside of him attempting somehow to remold his features.

No longer handsome, he was hideous.

"Velma!" cried Frank.

"I'm in here," she answered weakly. She turned to open the door.

Max darted. Nathan lunged, tripped and fell on all fours.

Max grabbed one of Nathan's fingers, bit it to the bone, shook it like a field rat, then let it go quickly before the other hand could close on his neck.

But Nathan had made progress. He was almost to the main ladder.

"Velma," called Frank, "I'm coming in!"

Henry's face poked through the opening. "Doc?"

"Lock the hatch, Henry!"

"But what about . . . ?"

Henry turned his head quickly, saw Nathan's huge face.

And Nathan screamed.

The hatch slammed tight. Slammed and was locked by its huge exterior bolt as Henry prayed for help.

And as Frank and Velma stood in the aft cabin doorway, Nathan went totally berserk. He began to kick and smash everything within reach. As if expendable, he bloodied and mauled his own hands and feet against wall fixtures, lamps, compasses, quadrants, calipers, bottles . . . anything.

While Max, poor Max, tried to hold his ground.

"Here, boy!" shouted Frank. "Come here!"

The dog's ears flattened. He paused, then limped quickly through the galley toward the open cabin door.

Frank reached out and pulled in Max by his collar, then shut and locked the mahogany door, hoping it would hold.

Nathan raged into the galley, bloody fists smashing cabinets, ravaging shelves, pounding plates to pieces, decimating glasses, mugs, cups, ripping, tearing, destroying, wreaking havoc on everything in his path. His mind ablaze:

I AM RAGE!

I AM TERROR!

I AM OBSCENE!

Hovering above the small gas stove, Nathan flung aside the simmering pot with birthing instruments, ripped an herb shelf from the wall, bashed pots and pans, knives and forks, colander and mixing bowls to the deck.

And in his delerium, he did not notice or care to notice the dry pine wood from the herb shelf lying shattered on the burner, or the gas flames that licked softly with little cat tongues.

Frank stood on a large sea trunk, unlugging the final brass bolt from the small overhead hatch.

Beyond the door, Velma listened to Nathan's tortured breathing.

Max growled.

None too soon, Frank loosened the hatch, for Nathan's gory fist smashed into the cabin, and Velma wailed like someone dying.

Frank reached down, lifted Velma to the trunk, grasped her by her slender waist and stuffed her into Henry and Anita's waiting arms.

Gulping a good breath of fresh air, Frank stepped away from the trunk, then hoisted Max, who still was snarling at the splintering door.

Frank pushed a wriggling Max up through the square brass-lined hole.

Using his hands like red fire axes, Nathan bludgeoned the mahogany paneling.

The door disintegrated. Smoke spilled into the cabin. An apparition of black and red lumbered through the smoke as if coughed up whole by a volcano.

Frank stood behind the trunk—the only thing between him and Nathan. Glowing eyes locked Frank in.

Frank had seen eyes shine like that before in snakes, lizards and alligators, but never in a man. And yet the man was not covered at all by slimy fungus.

Was Eric right? Could they adapt as quickly as they reproduced? Christ, the next thing you know they'd be smiling and reaching out like politicians just to shake your hand. One good handshake and everybody belongs to the same party!

But still there was something human in Nathan. There had to be.

"Nathan! Nathan! For God's sake, man!"

Yes, those yellow eyes cleared, softened somehow.

Somewhere inside Nathan, different forces struggled for absolute control, for absolute power over the universe. They fought a ritual battle of universal symbols amid neurons, arteries and spewing glands.

Nathan saw a butterfly-winged angel wrestle with a giant reptile. And each time the angel attempted to fly, the great serpent lashed more tightly about its puny legs, dragged it down

197

farther into a battlefield of primordial mud, shook it unmercifully, squeezed it, and in a final bloody rage, bit off its golden wings.

The serpent then screamed its joy and glared at Frank through Nathan's eyes.

Frank backed up in shock.

Anita stared speechless through the overhead hatch.

Nathan gazed upward with his bloody, grinning face, his cold, moonlight eyes, and his large hand snatched a strand of blond angel hair that trickled down from heaven. He yanked it.

Anita jerked backward, ripping the hair from her scalp.

Nathan moaned, rubbed the hair, sniffed its perfumed hormones, tasted it with keen senses, then crooned upward toward the flashing stars.

Deliverance! Deliverance!

All pity for Nathan gone, Anita stood above the monster, an absolute monster, one that needed her body to procreate. She would drown herself and her baby if he touched her.

Frank backed up to the end of the cramped cabin. He saw a diving mask, flippers, fishing rods. Christ, yes! He pulled an old spear gun from the pile of equipment.

Quickly he shoved the handle into his belly and drew back the slingshot that could hurl a spear into Nathan's mutant heart.

But the salt-rotted rubber snapped, breaking against his fingers.

Frank cursed. He thrust the gun before him like a bayonet. But he had no room to maneuver. He was forced to crouch between the narrowing deck and the overhead.

Nevertheless, Frank prepared to attack, to knock Nathan down, to stab him, to kill him in any way possible. But the horror of it was that *he* could become another Nathan. That he could be the one to contaminate his own wife.

"Nathan . . . Nathan!" called a high-pitched voice from the doorway, in grotesque sexual parody.

Velma.

Skinny little Velma stood in the smoke with her hands on her narrow hips, trying not to cough.

"Nathan! Nathan!" she cried again.

"Come here, Mr. Monster! Over here! Come!"

Velma backed up slowly. "I know what you want, monster. I know."

The two were in lock step now, moving toward the main hatch.

"But I don't think you're man enough to get it," added Velma angrily. "No!" she shrieked. "I don't think you're man enough!"

Velma touched the ladder to make sure it was there. To make sure she could escape this ghoulish nightmare.

Nathan's feet plodded forward like chummed fish bait, leaving bloody tracks behind him. He is close enough, thought Velma. Maybe too close. Can I still make it up the ladder? Is Doc free yet? Oh, my God.

"Now," called Frank from the open main hatch.

Stunned, Velma looked upward, saw Frank's hand reaching for hers. She raised her hand. She pushed away and was lifted—no, flew upward, outward, into the night.

Nathan stumbled forward through thickening smoke, narrowly missing Velma's sandaled foot, then turned blazing eyes on his persecutors.

And trembling, Frank locked Nathan into the oven.

Frank straightened. He stared up at the lifeboat on the forward deck.

"If Nathan breaks through, we abandon ship. Let's get ready."

The smoke was building. Nathan's breath came in short, choppy stabs to his lungs. Through the dense smog, he could see a faint reddish glow and he felt like any swamp animal feels when winter fires sweep across dry grass plains, hew hundred-foot cypresses to the ground and burn on for months because the flames survive deep down in the floating peat.

So Nathan cried out in a loud voice. And like a wild animal caught in a death trap, he pummeled the hatchway.

The moon was exceptionally bright, stars by the millions. Very little breeze in the sails.

On the forward deck, four people worked frantically to put a dinghy into black water that danced with phosphorescence about the motor sailer's fiber glass hull. Stars and plankton reflected infinity like mirrors opposed. As old as life itself, the plankton. Older, much older, the stars that had given them life.

And through this night a large dog barked. A goat baaed. Chickens screeched. And fists pounded against wood.

An insanity of sounds.

Frank readied the metal locks and snapped the oars into

place. He and Henry struggled to lift the heavy dinghy and slide it into the deep water.

Velma, meanwhile, opened the forward sea chest built into the deck itself and extracted one large package marked "SYNTHESIZER," another labeled "SURVIVAL."

She yanked them out and lay them on the deck beside Anita, who was now on all fours, breathing hard, trying to stay in charge of her own body, trying now to hold back the event they'd been hoping for for five barren years.

Nathan heard the dog barking outside. He wanted to strangle the dog, to tear it apart, strip it slowly limb from limb, chew out its guts with his teeth, tear away groin and testicles, peel off its furry skin.

Nathan threw his shoulder into the wooden hatch. Fire kissed his bare feet, bit curly black hair from his dark legs and urged him on. Again. Heave. Smash! Again. Again!

Once, twice, three times and the heavy door split from its hinges.

Max backed off, warily.

Smoke billowed from the cabin, fire racing close behind. And Nathan came crawling. Up the ladder. Onto the deck. Silently cursing the dog before him.

Frank helped Anita down into the dinghy. Henry stood in the boat, trying to steady it as Anita wobbled to her seat, reaching behind for the gunnels, head lowered, teeth against teeth, gritted.

"Hurry! Hurry!" someone said. And the dinghy rolled back and forth dangerously.

Max, like a pit fighter gone too many rounds, slipped on his bad leg. Nathan grabbed his neck and squeezed.

Max bit Nathan's hand, then cried out in pain. Anita looked up. Saw Nathan lift up Max by the collar. Saw him hurl the dog far into the ocean.

Glancing over her shoulder at Nathan, Velma handed Henry the heavy synthesizer box. Frank threw in the survival kit. The deck vibrated.

His clothes smoking, Nathan charged.

"Push off, Henry!" ordered Frank.

Henry fumbled with the oar and shoved away from the motorsailer.

"Jump!" Frank called to Velma. "Jump!"

"I'm afraid!" she screamed.

"Hold my hand!" cried Frank.

They leaped together into the abyss and cold salt water shocked their bodies, filled their nostrils and stung their eyes.

Nathan flung himself forward. He landed on the deck alone, his flesh burning.

Frank put his arm over Velma's shoulder and, sidestroking, swam toward the dinghy.

Not far away, Max also swam toward the dinghy, paddling with his head just barely above the water, the cast dragging him under.

"Don't struggle. I've got you," said Frank to Velma.

"Stay up, Max! Stay up!" cried Henry in tears.

Anita watched everything through a graying filter of total exhaustion. She saw one of the shadowy people spread his elongated arms above his head and wail at the moon like a werewolf. She saw fire sparkle from his shirt to his fingertips. She saw flames well up fiery red in the cabin portholes, the entire boat swirling in smoke, incendiary flickers racing up the sails and the poor damned soul screaming and screaming . . . screaming in the wilderness.

Then there was a bright flash against Anita's face. A loud explosion. A void opened enticingly. And as Anita's eyes closed in sleep, she felt herself falling, falling, falling like Alice down her long, spiraling hole into soft, cosmic blackness.

CHAPTER TWENTY-FIVE

A morning sun caressed the white beach, showing off its sculpture of ripple marks and bleached driftwood.

Sea gulls and willets raced squawking across the blue sky.

The ocean was calm. Sandpipers scurried down wet sand as gentle waves receded. The birds stopped and started abruptly, like silent-movie actors. They pecked at the sand, then hurried on.

A blue-green dragonfly paused motionless on the handle of an oar protruding from a dinghy named *Edith's Joy II*. The dinghy sat high on the beach; behind it—footprints on either side—a trail from the waterline.

The sea gull cry faded into the distance. And a new cry could be heard, the sonancy of the birds briefly intermingled with the cry of a human baby.

Large dunes unfolded, giant loaves weaving grasses in the light breeze.

Just over these dunes, and nestled in a bed of palmetto leaves, lay Anita with her newborn cradled in her arms, a rough lean-to of palm leaves erected for shade.

Frank, his shirt off, sat by Anita's side, staring with delight at his new child—a naked little girl.

Max sat at Anita's feet, yawning, sporting a new white cast of sticks and adhesive tape.

Anita took the baby to her breast. The tiny mouth stopped crying and suckled hungrily.

Frank stroked his wife's shining hair.

Farther down the beach, not far from its cocoon, a newly formed tiger swallowtail clutched the bark of a live oak tree and dried its fragile wings in the sun. The butterfly was beautifully marked in black and yellow, with a delicate sweeping tail at the bottom of each secondary wing.

Suddenly the insect fluttered to life, catching the ocean air currents under its wings. And with no fanfare was aloft, flying straight up, swooping, banking and laughing at the white earth, the blue-green sea, and the now-distant coppice of oak trees festooned with fresh, green moss.

It danced, twirled and spun to the music of warm sunlight, and of course was surprised to find itself in the shadow of a feathered wing.

With instinct born of survival, it dropped quickly and the black skimmer, foraging food for its newly hatched chicks, missed breakfast by less than an inch, snatching only a small piece of yellow wing.

Terrified, the butterfly dove straight down to ground level, where the water met the sand, and the sand clutched a gnarled piece of driftwood. There it sat on the silvered wood, resting and preparing its next move, when two human beings walked toward it.

Henry looked at the driftwood, then came close to the butterfly, which was opening and closing its wings slowly, testing them for takeoff.

"That's a tiger swallowtail," exclaimed Henry, who used to collect butterflies.

Velma nodded.

They moved on, Velma humming one of Anita's songs to herself above the waves. Henry, quite self-conscious still, having made some important discovery about life, as to how he might fit into the scheme of things.

Velma, the wind blowing her curly hair back, walked beside him and smiled out to sea.

Henry picked up a flat rock, rounded and smooth, and skimmed it out over the calm surf. It skipped three times across the water before sinking.

Proud of his toss, he turned to Velma. His grin was "aw, shucks"—spontaneous and disarming.

And for the first time in her life, Velma really and truly smiled back at Henry. It was an exquisite, almost maternal smile that added substance, even mystery to her open, freckled face.

"Good one, Henry!" she said and began to dance to her song, leaving small footprints in the sand behind her.

> "Oh, the colors of rainstorms
> Oh, the colors of sea
> Be bold with faint colors
> When you're thinkin' of me."

MISSION TO THE HEART STARS   57968-5/$1.95
In this sequel to THE STAR DWELLERS, the Angels, a tremendous energy form, have signed a treaty with humans. But their peaceful co-existence is threatened when a civilization at the center of the galaxy tries to make earth a "subject state."

TITANS' DAUGHTER   56929-9/$1.95
Sena, the blond blue-eyed heroine, is a tetrapoid giantess—taller, stronger, longer-lived, than "normal" men and women. For Sena, who was not yet thirty, the whole world was in the throes of an endless springtime of youth that would last more than a century. But would the jealous "normals" let her live?

AND ALL THE STARS A STAGE   41186-5/$1.50
When the sun explodes, all life will end. No one will survive the blow-up; except the men and women who crowd into a few starships and fly away into space while there is still time, to look for a new home in the infinite void, a new planet on which to settle.

VOR   44966-8/$1.95
Lt. Marty Petrucelli, Civil Air Patrol, USAF, was a bright young man with a troubled marriage, average ambition but an uncanny perception. How was he to persuade the experts of an Atomic Age that the monster poisoning the countryside with radiation was easily within their control?

Available wherever paperbacks are sold, or directly from the publisher. Include 50¢ per copy for postage and handling; allow 6-8 weeks for delivery. Avon books, Mail Order Dept., 224 West 57th St., N.Y., N.Y. 10019

2 Blish 12-82

If you like Heinlein, will you love Van Vogt?

A READER'S GUIDE TO SCIENCE FICTION

by Baird Searles, Martin Last, Beth Meacham, and Michael Franklin

Here is a comprehensive and fascinating source book for every reader of science fiction — from the novice to the discerning devotee. Its invaluable guidance includes:

* A comprehensive listing of over 200 past and present authors, with a profile of the author's style, his works, and other suggested writers the reader might enjoy

* An index to Hugo and Nebula Award winners, in the categories of novel, novelette, and short story

* An outstanding basic reading list highlighting the history and various kinds of science fiction

* A concise and entertaining look at the roots of Science Fiction and the literature into which it has evolved today.

"A clear, well-organized introduction."
Washington Post Book World

"A valuable reference work." Starship

AVON Paperback

46128-5 / $2.95

GSciFI 12-82